II.
LEAFMEAL
LIES

'What is our consciousness but a continual segue between our present and our past'

Janice Ball

Cover Picture
Wittenham Clumps by Janice Ball

First published in 2019 by Parkwall Press.

ISBN 978-1-5272-4523-5

To my Family and Friends
Written for Phil Ball

Contents

1 In Leafmeal Lies – Jacqueline

'La Butte'[1] de Lauzerte catches the slant of the mid-morning October sun and stands alone, proud and glistening, above the more subdued setting of the surrounding undulating farmlands. On its side there drapes and spreads the small town of Lauzerte, ascending, from the newer rendered houses with their tended gardens lower down, to the ancient, compact stone cluster above. At the very top, like a tarnished, ancient crown, rests 'La Cité Mediévale' – a silent, wise survivor and witness of the savagery, the plots and the intrigues of 'La Guerre de Cent Ans'[2] – now reduced to a tourist attraction.

La Cité is no longer a throbbing political nerve centre, nor one of commercial or social vitality, but thousands of tourists flock here each summer, picking their way through winding, narrow lanes and trampling on smooth, worn, cobbled streets into La

---

[1] Butte – an isolated hill with steep sides and a flat top – a smaller version of a mesa

[2] The Hundred Years' War

Place des Cornières. They chat incessantly as they industriously and superficially attempt to glean each bit of history from every worn stone wall.

By autumn, when the summer on-rush of tourists has abated, the residents reclaim their town. Once again there is a calm and normality here that is found in most small towns in the Midi-Pyrénées. People move more slowly and speak more softly than the hordes of gushing, marauding, camera-clicking, selfie posing visitors at the height of summer. If there are excitement and adventure in their lives, they are lived within the thick walls of their homes.

The sky often lours with heavy clouds in mid-October here or, at times, grey, still mist and fog may linger all day long. Not infrequently, howling, gusty wind may also rampage across this corridor between the Mediterranean and the Atlantic. This day, however, has turned out bright and warm, reaching a good 18°C before mid-morning. This does not surprise the locals. They embrace the changeable weather as a long missed friend or bear with it as a hardship that would soon pass. *'Mais ce n'est pas rare,'*[1] they would philosophise, having accepted that they are affected not only by the Mediterranean and the Atlantic, but also that they live within the shadows of the Pyrénées to the South and the Massif Central to the North.

Halfway up the town on Rue de la Barbarcane, on a small, dark, covered balcony, opened on one side only

---

[1] But this is not rare

and flushed with the front of the ancient stone house, Jacqueline sits, in the shade rather than towards the sun. A bowl of black coffee and a day old croissant lie on a small marble-top guéridon[1] with a moulded cast iron pedestal. It is probably a relic of some noisy bar in the region where once it would have stood in a corner or perhaps in front of a worn, velour covered sofa, with the marble cured into a greasy sheen by the curling and lazy fumes of cheap cigarettes and harsh cigars. On this guéridon, there now rests also a closed copy of *'The Sandgrown'un – My Whispers'*.[2]

The little balcony opens from her bedroom and provides a cosy, secluded area for her – secluded only from the occasional passer-by on the narrow lane below. Beyond the pale green, wooden balcony rails stretches a panoramic view of rooftops, of the farms and orchards far below and, hazily, of the distant woodlands.

The first time she stood on this balcony, Jacqueline was moved not so much by the distant views as by the geometric patchwork of crusty rooftops, which scaled unsteadily down to the centre of the town, with the upper floor of the Hotel Restaurant du Quercy just visible below.

She marvelled at the texture and subtle blend of colours of the arched roof tiles – from smoky greys to slate blue, from speckled russet to dull red, which

---

[1] A small round-top occasional table with a pedestal

[2] Will be made clear in Chapter 4

merged into seared heather with the occasional glints of flecks of weathered mica catching the eye. Some giant hands seemed to have taken hold and stretched across the roofs in some distant past and given them a double twist to disarrange them into a more artistic and organic display of angles and curves and undulation.

For one moment she wished she could paint, just as at some time or other she had wished she could play a musical instrument or sing a song. But she was distracted. Emanating from the buildings huddled together below was a very faint, warm smell of cooking, of garlic and onions and herbs, all hinting of human activity, of hidden lives, of feelings. She turned around to look again at the solid stone walls of the house. They should keep the house cool in the summer and hold out the cold in the winter. Away from the centre of the town and La Cité, she thought, she would not be too much within the tourist circus and yet not be too cut off. And the house was small and cosy, requiring the minimum of upkeep. It would not be a bad place to be, to be alone.

Jacqueline is neither lonely for new company nor for new experiences, although the knowledge of living among people rather than in stone-cold isolation comforts her. There is already a surfeit of the past, trapping and drawing in each of her thought like a tenaciously sticky web, for her to require new facets to her life. There is nostalgia though for the life that has already been. Nostalgia for that someone familiar, perhaps, who could glance at her and understand immediately the nuance on her face, the way she thinks and the way she reacts. She misses having someone who exists within the same equation, thus making their history together the present instead of the past – a continuum instead of a dead end.

Little recollections flash frequently through her mind of the people who are gone from her life – the pain they had caused, the shattering passion and love, and the brief moments of hope that each might have engendered and then failed to deliver. So she sits on the balcony, or in the restful Jardin du Pèlerin[1] nearby, or takes long walks and often travels the world but, always, the adventure, the turmoil, the glimpses of pleasure and sagacity are resourced from within her. All present activities are simply for the passing of time. And time seems interminable when it is no longer a necessity – when it is expendable.

She no longer notices the rooftops or the burnt stubbles of sunflowers in the distant fields, or the fine white nettings that are stretched over the apple orchards beyond and hardly, the occasional sun-baked farm house dotted within that expanse called a view. These days her glazed eyes see inwards rather more than seeing out and it has become increasingly more difficult for her to concentrate even on books she loves. The books she reads are the books of her past – old

---

[1] Pilgrim's Garden. Lauzerte is on the pilgrimage route of the Santiago de Compostela

friends. New books hold little interest for her for she can find no link to excite her.

Picking up the coffee cup and the half eaten croissant, she enters the house. From her bedside table she picks up a small bottle of Chanel 5 and automatically dabs the inside of the glass lid on her left wrist, expertly upon the pulse, and goes downstairs to the kitchen. Glancing briefly in a small oval hallway mirror, she adjusts her hair grips and then puts on a light cardigan hanging by the door and, slinging a printed jute shopper over a shoulder, she leaves the house.

She turns the corner into Rue du Potevin and walks down the first flight of steps to the pharmacy, which is located to the right of a small terraced area. She collects a prescription and, coming out again, finds herself above the next flight of steep, wide, descending steps, bathed in the warmth of the sun on her face and through the thin woollen sleeves of the cardigan, on her arms. She stands uncertainly for a moment and closes her eyes. The weak October sunlight flushes upon her lids. She shivers, seemingly moved by some recollection of her past.

'Close your eyes now,' he said, wrapping around her from behind, 'close your eyes and feel.'

She closed her eyes, nervously vulnerable, afraid that she might fail. He had told her that people tended to rely too much on just what they could see. 'We have other senses, you know,' he said.

She was conscious of a faint perfume of soap from his body. By then she knew that it must be from a bar of Lux in a green plastic tray at the foot of the bath in his flat. Then there was the masculine undertone of cigarette and wine and muskiness. At least she thought it was musk. Musk, she had learned from a girl school friend, was a male smell. It was the essence of their magnetism. It was a disturbing smell, not particularly pleasant but somehow, unquestioningly relevant, she decided.

His breathing, as he bent over her head, tickled her hair and she felt the soft pressure of his arms around her. He did not crush her as she thought men would when they held a girl, because they were strong and would make a girl breathless and faint. He was firm but inclusive, running his arms alongside hers like equal partners. 'No,' she told herself, 'extend your field away from him. This is not what he means.'

'There's the breeze – in my hair and on my face. Somewhere there is a bon-fire, I can smell it. That's a car passing by on the bridge, and ...and I can hear a duck. I can't smell the river – I thought I might. But I can hear the heavy fall of the water at the weir. I think someone is saying something to the lock-keeper. Is that the lock gate opening? And I can feel you,' she finally admitted timidly but coquettishly.

She could hear her heart beat and thump and wondered if he noticed it. He must – he seldom missed a thing.

Her summer frock, in pale green poplin with a motif of tiny pairs of leaves in a darker shade, hung lightly upon her, so softly against the scantly noticeable rise and fall of her breasts. Her mother had bought the fabric and pattern in New York and had sewn it for her for a tea dance at the Goring Parish Hall[1] three months before. It had become her favourite frock because it was there that they had first met. She wondered if he liked the way it fitted her right to the waist before billowing out in a circular cut, catching the light breeze from the river. These thoughts she did not share with him. And it was months later that she discovered that he had not liked the frock at all, or at least he had grown not to like it on her. She was no longer a little girl, he said, a woman now. There was no need for puffed sleeves and sashes.

'My name is Gérard,' he said, with a slight nod of the head, as he approached her from across the room, 'and what is yours?'

'Jacqui. How do you do?' she said shyly, glad of the crowd and the noise and the loud music in the hall which seemed to have offered her a degree of protection. It would have been an unbearable embarrassment if he had walked towards her when she was on her own. She would have felt exposed, not knowing how to sit, where to put her arms, how to cross her legs – an ungainly butterfly emerging from its chrysalis uncertain of how to spread its wings.

---

[1] Now known as The Goring Village Hall at Goring-on-Thames

Although she got on well enough with the boys at school, she was fundamentally shy, conscious of her developing body but knowing well that the boys had eyes only for the more obviously outgoing and physically more mature and attractive girls. She had never considered herself as pretty but had not let that pre-occupy her. She assumed that at some stage there would be a boy, that she would get married and have a family. These were the order of things.

But here was a man. He had encroached into her space. He had asked her to dance. She had demurred. No, she did not know how to dance, not the fast dances, no. He had insisted.

'It is not a problem, Jacqueline,' he assured her, 'We will do it slowly.'

He led her on the slowest dance ever. She laughed because it was ridiculous – it would have been, at least, if one of the boys had suggested it. He was a grown man and in control. It was funny. They danced a slow, slow fox-trot to the upbeat of Connie Francis and Bill Hayley and then fell into steps with *Blueberry Hill*. Then, letting go of her, he went into an exaggerated jive. 'Come on, come on,' he shouted, 'have some fun, M'moiselle.'

'M'dame'

'Bonjour, m'sieur, dame'[1] she replies, shading her eyes to see who they are.

---

[1] Good day, sir, madam

'Au marché?'

'Mai oui, comme toujours en mercredi,'

'On doit manger – j'suppose hein!'[1]

Wednesday is the day of the petit marché fermiers[2] at la place du Foirail. There is a much larger market at La Place des Cornières on Saturdays, but Jacqueline has found the Wednesday market more manageable and sufficient for her usual needs. She continues down the next flight of steps, a few steps behind monsieur and madame Martel, who are neighbours from a street further up the hill.

Although she is known and accepted locally, it is no more than on the basis of a few greetings and pleasantries. The people of the town refer to her as 'l'anglaise' or 'la dame anglaise' and even 'madame Jacqueline' rather than 'madame Wyndham'. They enjoy guessing how 'Wyndham' should be pronounced, but decided it was probably more polite and safer to leave it as madame or Jacqueline when addressing her.

When she first moved to the town there had been debate about her of course. She had stood out among some women *of a certain age* who, as fashion had become redundant with age gave way sensibly to the acquisition of comfort. They could see that she stood tall in expensive trousers or straight skirts, and that her

---

[1] To the market?   But yes, as always on a Wednesday.   One must eat – I suppose eh!

[2] The small farmers' market

coats in winter were comfortable but well-tailored. Although not young, she carried herself straight and maintained a trim figure. Obviously from a city, they would remark.

Who was she, why had she come to live at Lauzerte, was she a widow, how old was she, were there children who visited, who was the gentleman who had called on her, was she an English eccentric? To all these Jacqueline would not have volunteered answers, but then she has never been asked these questions. There is certain aloofness about her, even when she smiles and tries to be amiable, that does not invite familiarity.

That she is English and probably a widow or divorcée has been established by Sophie, a thirty-something English speaking assistant at l'office du tourisme[1] who had originally suggested *Le Nid d'Or*[2] to her as suitable for one or two occupants on a long term arrangement. The owner, being of ill health, had moved out to be with her son at Montauban.

A dozen or so stalls, mainly of local farm produce, fill the Place du Foirail. It is a small market catering mainly for the townspeople and can get busy in the morning. Shoppers and vendors chat to each other familiarly. Laughter rings out with the good humoured bargaining that goes on. The scene would not be complete without a few older men speaking in low voices while smoking their pipes or cigars.

---

[1] Tourist Office
[2] The Golden Nest

Top on her shopping list is wild mushroom: cep and chanterelle and morel that are displayed in simple baskets or trays. Then she picks a large head of lettuce and a few tomatoes before moving on to select 2 small goat's cheese. After deciding on 150gms of jambon cru[1], she heads off to the boulangerie across the road for a baguette and 4 thick slices of bread sliced from an enormous loaf resting on a trestle.

This is the simple pattern of her diet at home. A large handful of wild mushrooms, for instance, fried quickly in olive oil with a pinch of salt and served on toast make a light but filling meal for her. Or she might make an omelette, adding some sliced mushroom while the omelette is still 'baveuse'[2]. She would break a leaf of sage or crumble a small twig of thyme into it before serving it with some salad. At the market, she often finds little fresh bouquets garnis which she loves to have in the kitchen, using them not as a bouquet but picking different bits for different purposes as they dry and concentrate their flavour.

Although she seldom cooks meat, except perhaps for grilling a confit of cuisse de canard[3], she delights in the large variety of jambon cru available here, which she savours, accompanied by a glass of red wine and good, locally baked, wholemeal bread.

---

[1] Cured ham

[2] Runny

[3] Confit of duck leg

She drinks her wine now as Gérard used to do – as an essential part of a meal, to add depth to the flavours, to stretch the meal and to degrease the fat. Gérard, growing up at Montgiroux in Mayenne [1], was introduced to wine from an early age. However, he took the regional wine as a matter of course, seldom experimenting with wine from other regions of France and especially not from other countries. When he moved to England in the late 1950s, he lamented the lack of choice of wine there, although he actually tasted more French wine from different regions of France than he had when he was at home.

He had introduced her to wine, but it was Michael, many years on, who made it into a sophistication, explaining the subtlety of flavours, how the weather and soil conditioned the varieties and how to match the richness or lightness of certain food with certain wine. These days, any regional red wine would pass muster with her and she finds it calms her and stretches her meagre meals a little over long afternoons and, when evening falls, it helps her to cope with the relentlessly long hours before she could fall asleep.

Jacqueline hurries home from the market, climbing the familiar flights of steps with practised ease. David has said that he would be there at 11 and he is unlikely to be late. She changes into a pair of slate brown MaxMara trousers, tops it with a fitted orange T-shirt and selects an un-bleached cotton jacket in case the

---

[1] Mayenne is in the Pays de la Loire, France

weather turns. She looks forward to seeing David again. He is her one link with the past, the one person who could rouse her from her stupor, and she finds herself waiting eagerly for his arrival. She has reserved a table at *Le Vinois* at Caillac for 1pm and anticipates an intimate lunch mixed with business matters they have to discuss.

David would find some place to park his car lower down the town and walk up to *Le Nid d'Or*. On his first visit, she had given him specific instructions on where he could park and that he should get there before *les heures de repas*[1] so he could ask Sophie at l'office du tourisme on how he could find her house. If it had been Michael, she told herself, he would have researched in good time and knew exactly how to get to her. Had it been Carl ...his instinct, dear, dear Carl, would have brought him to her. But David – he would have left everything to chance and lose his way before finally stumbling upon her. That was not without its charm, she considered, but it would have ruffled her if he had turned up late.

Charm is something David has in plenty, all the more disarming because it comes so naturally. Warm and jovial and kind, he never has to work at being liked. With little claim to any intellectual or emotional profundity, he has been by nature, Jacqueline concludes, a loyal and devoted friend on whom she has leant in all ways during the past few years. To give him

---

[1] Lunch hours

credit, she smiles musingly as she waits now, he has not been late to see her here before.

In fact David flew into Rodez the previous day. He would have stayed the night normally at Cahors, but since they are having lunch at Caillac, so close to Cahors, it makes no sense for him to drive to Lauzerte only to drive back to Caillac and then repeat that journey. So he had driven a little further and found a charming auberge[1] among the hills on the Chemin de Pignols outside of Moissac. He left the auberge soon after breakfast, driving around the area, making sure that he is at Lauzerte in good time. He has not seen her for five months now and he wants the meeting to go well. He parks his car way before time and trudges up to La Place des Cornières and has a cup of coffee in the square.

Sitting quietly on his own in a square anywhere in the world is not a scenario familiar to him. He is gregarious and requires the re-assurance of family and friends around him. Yet he is willing to give quiet corners of the world a try as long as there is Jacqueline. He knows that she travels for weeks and months at a time, often to obscure places in India or South America or in Asia, away from the glitter and vibrancy of city life. With this he would gladly have to learn to cope. Unlike Jacqueline though, he finds all the climbing, even at Lauzerte, a little taxing and is glad that he would be walking down towards her house.

---

[1] An inn or tavern

He wants to time it just right. He will not allow any misunderstanding to impair their time together. Who knows better than he how little it takes to veer the path of life away from where it is intended. Just a few words, a little slip, a missed opportunity and hey presto, you are on a different trajectory and may not even know what you have missed.

This is his time. He will have patience. It is not in his nature to ponder long and deeply over any issue. He gauges what is immediately ahead of him and responds accordingly. He is an opportunist rather than a schemer. But with Jacqueline, he knows he must plan and he must probe, if he wants to be a permanent part of her life. Exactly how he will go about this he has no idea. In the past few years he had regained a youthful, male confidence and pride in her reliance on him. He was by her side when she needed him. He was her confidant and her saviour if not quite her salvation. Now he wants more than that. He wants to be the 'Michael' in her life.

Le Nid d'Or seems to rise from one huge granitic block to its right, which could, quite appropriately, be called the corner stone. The house itself, built of large but irregular blocks of square and rectangular stones, seems to have emerged directly from the hill behind it. Three paved steps lead to the sturdy brown-stained wooden door of horizontal planks held together by iron studs. David pauses, bracing himself, as if the purpose of his visit has only just begun. He is about to knock on the door when he hears Jacqueline coming out of the narrow but high wooden gate of the small, walled side garden. She extends both her hands to him, smiling, and looks at him before embracing him.

'David, David,' she utters.

She has changed, David notices. What was once her glossy, dark brown hair, which would display highlights of red when light shone on it, has now lost its sheen from too much sun. She has recently allowed the grey to show through in patches around the crown and temples and in finer veins along its length. The glow and youthfulness of her face have now faded and the lines on her forehead and at the corners of her mouth have deepened and gradually become pronounced. In five months, he has seen so much change. How could he bear to leave her at the end of the day?

'I see you are ready to go,' he said, resting his hands on her shoulders. If there is such a thing as an aura, then there is an aura of deep and enveloping friendship between them. They walk briskly downhill to the car, turning round to smile at each other now and again. She feels relaxed in his company, comfortable with his comprehension of the person that she is. A friendship that goes back over 30 years, she evaluates, is worth more than any passion – well, at least when that passion is but an incorporeal memory. 'Passion!' it occurs to her, with a shrug of the shoulders.

She had a quick shower, she remembers, and stepped into fine, black lace knickers and bra, which she had specially bought for the trip. She looked into the mirror and thought she still looked good, though a little tired. All the same, she decided to switch off the bathroom light before stepping out into the dark room. At first the room seemed pitch black, but her eyes soon adjusted and she could perceive sharp points of light from the setting sun through the gaps in the volets[1].

A little longer and she could see him half lying on the bed, with one leg stretched out and the other slightly bent. A classic statuesque pose, she recalls now. Once again she almost gasped, as she had often done when they first became lovers, at how attractive he was. She had begun to perspire again in the heat and humidity of the late afternoon. If he had wanted to make a fresh start, to re-vitalise their flagging ardour, then he had succeeded.

She had agreed to come with him to Champagne out of a sense of fairness, to see if her own awakened passion for Carl could be transferred to him, to see if they could save their relationship, to see if it was enough to have forgiven. Seeing him lying there with the light from the volets diffusing in a warm sheen on him, re-kindled in her the rousing, sacrificial expectation of offering her body to him.

She recalled the garçonnière in Marguerite Duras's 'L'Amant de la Chine du Nord'[2] – a small bachelor flat which rich Chinese families would install for their

---

[1] Shutters
[2] The Lover From North China

sons, where they could experience and experiment with women, sow their wild oats, be kept in check from that irresponsible thing called love, before being arranged into a marriage – a marriage of convenience which could provide him with sons and in turn fulfil his filial duties by providing his parents with grandsons.

She walked up to him. She would be sacrificed. He could be the predator and she the prey. She must separate that moment from the adulteration of the past and any anticipation of the future. She would keep that moment pure – make that moment entire. She would give them another chance. She would provoke and inflame his lust and allow him to quell hers. That moment had to be kept entirely physical. She was tired of thinking, forever thinking. Forever asking – Why? Why? Michael, Michael.

'Michael!'

'Sorry?' David reacts, turning towards her.

'Oh, I'm sorry, David. I was just thinking about Michael,' she apologises. After a long pause, she continues. 'You remember when we went off to Champagne that August? I wanted so badly to work things out, and it was promising at the beginning. I understood his position and made as much allowances as I could. Like a bird with a damaged wing, he was unable to fly… not able to fly. We failed each other.'

David is surprised that she has brought up the subject of Michael. They have not spoken of him except where absolutely necessary. They are bound eternally together, Jacqueline, Michael and he. He cannot change that, but has learned to manage the bitterness and regrets. He has learned to accept the status quo and, instead of regressing, looks towards the future. He is in no position to advise Jacqueline. He cannot play the exorcist and cast the devil out. She is entitled to her own suffering – deservingly so, many would say. Just let him be there with her to accompany her along this late journey, to be strong for her.

David's mood lifts a little when he sees how Jacqueline has enjoyed her lunch. When she goes out now, she prefers her meals to be fresh and light and takes pleasure in the skilful presentation of each dish. *Le Vinois* offers both culinary and visual excellence. When coffee is served, David goes to the car to fetch the legal documents which she has to sign.

'What did Josh think of my offer?' Jacqueline asks.

'Extremely touched that you have so much faith in him. He has asked me to thank you. We walked to the car park together from the solicitor's. He couldn't believe that you had been so generous to him and felt that it has set him up for the rest of his life – sort of given him a final sense of direction. You know his wife Tina is expecting again. I think he is a really genuine person. He will do your trust justice.'

'And Denise?' she asks knowingly. 'Tearful, I presume.'

'Yes,' David smiles, 'very much so. I suppose it has solved some of her problems and given her financial and career stability. And it must bolster her confidence.'

But not completely pleased, Jacqueline suspects. She can picture Denise, gushing with gratitude, relieved at her good fortune, but still dissatisfied and bitter about the injustice of her lot. She is the longest serving member of the team, but it is Josh who has been offered the largest share of the company. Jacqueline has felt that Josh would be the one with the driving force to take the company further. He is tougher and would not dither when confronted with decision making. Denise is excellent at her work but lacks the imagination and the ambition to use this opportunity as a spring-board to greater things.

Although she is taking leave of the business, Jacqueline wants to ensure that it survives under good hands. She has divided the shares into 3 parts: 40% to Josh, 30% to Denise and the remaining 30% to be shared by the rest of the staff while they remain with the company. She feels confident that Josh would have ways to garner the support of the other members of the staff even if Denise is in opposition. There is a darker, edgier side to Josh beneath his apparently quiet, acquiescent nature. She likes that in him. Although Denise would make the clients feel welcome, it is Josh who would instil confidence in them.

There was a time when Jacqueline had thought that Denise and she might have become friends. She understood the difficulty and stress of bringing up two young boys and was able and willing to assist in any way. However, she very soon found it hard to distinguish between Denise's facts and her sentiments. Denise was a woman of little nuances. Everything was 'utterly' or 'absolutely' or 'completely' so. Someone was either the kindest, the sweetest, the most intelligent, the best or the most hateful, the most selfish, the strangest. An opinion was constantly exaggerated and stated as a fact. Jacqueline grew wary and weary from this bombardment of superlative expressions and emotions. Her friendship could not root where there were so much fluffs and so little substance with so little else to compensate for them. It was a pity because she did not dislike Denise.

'There we are,' Jacqueline says with relief as she puts her signature to the last copy of the documents David has presented to her. 'I suppose I am finally free from all the ties back home. Thank you so much, David. I do not know how I could have sorted out everything without you.'

'I'm just sorry it has to come to this,' David replies.

'But you mustn't be. This is such a relief to me. It gets more and more irksome now for me to cope with responsibilities and obligations. Leaving the business is the sensible thing to do, and I couldn't have gone back to *Corner Oak* again. It took a long time but I'm glad you managed to sell it for me. What are the people like who bought the house?'

'Very good sort, really. They have just returned to England from Belgium with a young family – 2 boys and a girl, I believe. He's a CEO with an international transport company and Elaine is a nurse.'

Jacqueline smiles sadly and says, 'Well, *Corner Oak* deserves a happy family.'

'But what about you, David,' she continues, 'is your business still doing well at Pangbourne[1]?'

'Oh, yes. Gavin looks after it most weeks now. It has been a good move. It makes good sense to be close to both the M4[2] and M3[3] corridors. Judy takes care of the Barnet office and I feel sort of redundant. But that is what I want,' David explains – proud that his son and daughter have turned out to be responsible people and that he is able to provide for them.

'And Susan?' she enquired after his wife.

'Oh, Susan is enjoying working in the Barnet office. It gives Judy more time in her marketing role.'

'And you, are you happy, David?' she is tempted to ask, but decides to hold back. She does not have a heart generous enough at the moment to worry about him. He has his family, Jacqueline reasons, which is more than she has. He will be alright. He will never have the capacity for great depths of feeling and therefore great happiness, she thinks, but on the other hand, he would probably never experience great loss and pain. What a blessing that is. Surely, it is the reward for his goodness, she concludes, looking up and smiling at

---

[1] A small Thameside town in Berkshire

[2] Motorway 4 from London Westward to Bristol and Wales

[3] Motorway 3 from London in a Southwesterly direction to Southampton

him, treasuring the gentle affection that rises within her for him.

After lunch they stroll through the village and find a sentier[1] which leads through a lightly wooded area before emerging onto a quiet road with a vineyard on one side and some large modern properties on the other. Walking through vineyards gives Jacqueline a lift every time. She loves the order of the rows of vine contrasted with the gnarled and tortured dark stems, whether when bare in winter or lush with leaves in summer.

The story behind viniculture – the controlled pruning of the vine, the anticipation of the weather, the vendanges [2] with family or migrant labour, the communal repas[3], the crushing and production of wine, or champagne or brandy, the marketing of the finished products and the convoluted romance of dégustation[4] and the connoisseurs – fascinates her.

And then there is the story behind the rose bushes planted at intervals at the head of rows of vine to detect and forewarn of any disease before it spreads to the vine. Michael and she had enjoyed many happy hours walking through vine growing country. Of course, they were much, much younger then. And Carl... no, that was on the *Ridgeway*[5] back home. How

---

[1] Path

[2] The grape harvest

[3] Meals

[4] Tasting (of wine)

[5] An ancient walkway in Southern England

he had loved the woodlands and the open country. Just to get away from London. But no, she must not think of him. She cannot bear it, not now. Maybe when it is dark and she is alone. Maybe then she will think of him. Not now.

David realises that her attention is no longer there with him. Her thoughts have strayed. This happens more and more often now but he does not begrudge her these private moments. After all, he is physically there with her. It is, nonetheless, painful to watch someone who is normally so aware of her environ, so quick-witted, so responsive, becoming lost in a past which can only brew depression. He has learned in the last few years the art of keeping silent when he is with her. There is no compass to the wandering of her mind, but at least, often enough, she returns to him.

They walk for about an hour and then David drives her to Cahors where they have coffee on a terrace, watching people passing by, getting on with their lives, as daylight passes into night. He is reluctant to take her back to what he considers to be her prison, but which, to her, is the only haven in which she can survive on her own, undisturbed, unfettered by reality. Taking her back would also beckon their good-bye. He will walk her up to *Le Nid d'Or*. He will not go in. It would be too hard to tear himself away again.

It is already dark when they reach Lauzerte. David is surprised at her energy and nimbleness as she tackles the steep steps towards the house. As they approach the house, his resolve of not entering it weakens. If she asks, he argues, he could not possibly refuse.

'Come in and have a coffee before you leave,' she suggests. 'It would keep you awake for the long drive.'

She prepares the coffee for him. As usual there is never any milk in the house, but that is another thing he would have to get used to. Coffee keeps her awake, so she has a glass of red wine. He is offered an omelette, but settles for a sandwich. Why is jambon cru so chewy? He tries to eat it genteelly but finds himself swallowing it as quickly as he can. What an awful texture and taste! And there is no butter with it – just a little salad. Michael would have loved it, of course, but he, David, is not about to give any indication of his very restrictive, ingrained English palate.

'Would you be going away this year?' he asks.

'I've not decided, but I have been thinking of Tasmania to visit Clinger and from there Australia or even New Zealand. It would take some organising and I'm not up to it at the moment. I might just find something at the last minute. Well, it would actually be next year by then. What about you?'

'Oh, nowhere in particular. Susan likes somewhere sunny – Spain or the Canaries. I'll leave it to her. We try to spend Christmas as a family, but it gets more difficult each year. The children would probably have their own plans,' he replies. 'But you mustn't spend the winter and especially Christmas here on your own,' he adds.

It would be too depressing. This whole place, so dingy and quiet, would make anyone go barmy. He has never liked the place, finding it dark and cramped. There is a smokiness to the stone walls which makes the room dreary, even though the fireplace has not been used for a long time, having been blocked up and replaced by an electric fire. If he were here with her, it would be a different matter. For her to be alone with her morbid thoughts in the depth of winter would destroy her eventually.

'Oh, David, I'll be alright. I'm tough, you know. Stop worrying about me. Besides, I am now completely free and I'll stay if I am so inclined and leave whenever I want if I need some distraction. Life isn't so bad, you know, considering that we all have to pay our due.'

'Due suggests guilt. You are not guiltier than millions of people in the world who have made a mistake when confronted with unpleasant choices.'

He must be thinking about Carl, Jacqueline concluded. He so often gets the wrong end of the stick. However, if it is about Carl, 'Oh, it was no mistake,' she replied, 'how on earth do you think I can survive now without it? It's just that there is nothing left now, nothing to look forward to.'

But there is me. I'll be here for you. We'll travel together, reminisce together if you so wish, David wants to tell her, but knows it is the wrong time to make such suggestions. He has to settle his own affairs first in order to play a supportive role, but he couldn't envisage how to do that.

'I'm not too old to start again, under normal circumstances, you know, but everything of importance seems to be behind me. To think that everything that I had ever felt, ever done, have led towards this. You are the fortunate one of us all, you must recognize that. You have roots, a family...' she points out to him, but at the back of her mind lurks this judgment that it is, however, so much mediocrity. Wasn't it Carl who once said that he could not live with mediocrity?

David takes his leave soon after. Jacqueline has warned him that it could get foggy this time of the year. Besides, he does not want to overstay his welcome. There is little in common to talk about except the past, which he tries to avoid bringing up. If there is going to be a future for them, he must be with her on a permanent basis. It is a wrench for him to go, but he must go and quickly.

A sudden impulse takes hold of him and he embraces her and kisses her very tenderly on the lips – a little too prolonged to be casual. He promises to come back soon and departs, walking, down-heartedly, around the corner as she closes the door.

'Oh, Michael, Michael,' he cries, as he drives towards Moissac, 'what have you done to us all!'

Michael, the most beautiful person he had ever seen, striding ashore like a corny cliché from the sea. Even in the half light, the most beautiful being he had ever seen. That summer of 76, hot and sultry, promised never to end.

Michael's letter came on a Thursday. In those days David's parents owned a green-grocer's South of Uxbridge. During his college summer break he helped out at the shop as he was expected to do and for some pocket money. He was the baby of the family, being 10 and 6 years younger than his sister, Jean and his brother, Tony, respectively. It had always been assumed that Tony, who was not exceptionally good at school, would follow his father into the green-grocer trade. But David was to be different. He must go to college and maybe he could establish himself in some kind of profession. It would not be practical to have both brothers in one small business.

Tony went into the shop with his father early each morning and worked till just before noon, when his mother would come to take over and stay till three, so that he and his father could have a break and take in lunch.

That Thursday, his mother arrived as usual but with a letter for David. David knew immediately that it must be from Michael. He had never either written or received a letter before, and Michael had said he would write. During the previous college term, Michael had been surprised that David had never been out of England and had made him promise to apply for a passport. He would pick David up on his Yamaha and they could spend a week or so in France.

The passport was applied for and duly received, but David thought nothing more of it. People do say things at the excitement of the moment and then forget about them. Besides, close friends though they had become over the past year, it was a college friendship and Michael owed him no obligation.

Although his family were not poor, they were not sophisticated people, and David wondered if he would fit in with Michael's life style or expectation outside of College. Michael, who had travelled widely with his parents, who went to theatres and classical concerts, who dined at posh restaurants, who had a quiet arrogance about him, was surely out of David's league. So, although he instinctively knew the letter was from Michael, he was still surprised.

David made his excuses and retired to the storeroom at the back of the shop. There had been a delivery in the morning of crates of vegetables and oranges. The smell of citrus fruit would ever after remind him of reading Michael's letter that day. Yet, it was a very simple and short letter to the effect that he would be coming to pick David up on the following Tuesday morning at about 5 o'clock and that they would cross over to Calais on the ferry and have lunch and spend a few hours there before travelling westward along the coast. The decision was made for him. Michael had assumed that it was a fait accompli.

David found himself shaking, closing his eyes and trying to get a hold of himself. This short trip across the channel would be a big adventure. To be with Michael would make it doubly so. He was certain that his parents would let him go but he was a little more concerned with his finances. He had not saved very much from working at the shop and did not know how to ask his parents to fund his trip. In the end, it was Tony who came to the rescue. Having enquired about the trip and about Michael, he came up with £50. He would not have David's friend think that they were paupers.

David cannot remember exactly what they did that day except that he had tried oysters and experienced a platter of *fruits de mer*[1] for the first time. That evening, after dinner at a small bistro, where Michael urged him to try some French cheeses, and persuaded him to have some wine instead of beer, they rode off along the coast on Michael's four year old Yamaha YR5. He is vague now about the places they rode by but, around 10.30 that night, they stopped along a stretch of beach, somewhere between two headlands – with some names to do with the nose, if he remembers rightly – something *nez*[2] or other.

It had been hot the whole day and the evening was muggy and warm. Having travelled all day long they were tired and felt grimy. Michael stood his bike behind a dune and they found a sheltered spot to leave their bags. David lay on the sand, exhilarated at being abroad, at being gown up and independent. He turned

---

[1] Seafood

[2] Cap Blanc-Nez and Cap Gris-Nez

his head and saw Michael stripping. He closed his eyes and breathed in deeply the balmy, the glorious air.

'Come on,' Michael called out. He was already in the water, beckoning to David. The water felt cold to begin with but, as David began to swim, he gradually became accustomed to it. England is on an island, but he had never swum in the sea before. From the gentle light of the new moon, which had suddenly become apparent as the twilight waned, David could see Michael smiling. It was unusual to see him so carefree. There was a part of him always guarded from the world, which made him so interesting. Perhaps, being in the middle of nowhere, away from home and college and people, had put him at ease. They stayed in the water, David remembers, careless of time and responsibilities. Michael wanted to know what David thought of France.

'Don't know!' he said, 'but I am abroad and in France, that's good enough for me. I'm in France, I'm in France,' he yelled into the night air, splashing Michael in the face with water.

Michael told him about a concert of 20th Century composers he had attended in London and in reciprocation, David told Michael about Gloria, a girl from his old school, with whom he had met up again. Yes, Gloria, David recalls now, he'd not thought of her in years – lovely, beautiful girl. Done well for herself, he has heard – married advantageously to a top barrister in London.

David was drying himself when Michael stood in the shallows and stepped towards the shore. David couldn't take his eyes off him. He was tall and slim and walked with so much grace yet so manfully. His wet hair was so dark that instead of receding into the darkening sky, stood out against it and made his tanned face appear pallid. He laughed as David threw the towel to him, and David had to turn his eyes away, so full was his heart of gratitude and admiration. They slept on the beach that night, and when David woke in the early hours of the morning, as the sky began to lighten, he found that Michael had covered him with his jacket. Sitting up, he called and waved at Michael, who was standing dreamily at the water's edge.

For some reason, David felt that he had grown up overnight. He had Gloria, and he had the best of friends. He felt he understood the what-for of life. They rode on to Saint-Valery-sur-Somme that morning and then on to Honfleur, and that summer continued on and on and on, even until when they finally went back to college in September.

In September – ah, in September they met Jacqueline.

2 Watford Days – Michael and David

To Michael's annoyance, the 15.25 train arrived 10 minutes late, even though it had not surprised him. Very particular about time keeping, he wished that British Rail would occasionally prove him wrong in his expectation of their 'scheduled' delays.

'Hi mate!' David called out as he saw Michael. 'Alright?'

'David,' Michael responded. 'Give me that,' he said, pointing to the large travel bag, and taking it from him with a pat on his back.

'Hell! What's in here, books?' he exclaimed.

'No, my books are in the sports bag. Lots of food that my mum had packed,' David explained, laughing.

'You would've thought there are no shops around here,' Michael joined in.

'So, this new place, is it far?' David enquired, brimming with curiosity.

'Just 10 minutes' walk,' Michael replied. 'It's off St John's Road. You'll like it.'

Michael had got back a week earlier to look for a place for him and David to stay. The previous year had been a repugnant experience for him. They had shared a house with 2 other students quite close to college. Although he had been civil, he had found the messiness, the shallowness of conversation and the general loudness of his housemates quite insufferable.

Sharing a kitchen and a bathroom with them, he had explained to his parents, was a nauseous experience he could not tolerate for another year. Although David had been oblivious to the state of the house and had been perfectly happy to rub shoulders with his mates, Michael had kept to his bedroom as much as possible without appearing rude. Being overtly rude was not a characteristic his up-bringing would allow him to exhibit.

Owing to some quirk of nature Michael had befriended and taken a liking to David, who was nothing at all like him. David had nothing of the sophistication and the social grace that appeared to have come so naturally to Michael. David was impressionable and displayed an openness and an innocence which Michael had found engaging.

Shorter than Michael by a couple of inches and broader than he was, David was, nonetheless, not only attractive but also likable. Of the two of them, it was David who had the friends and the fun. Although Michael would not consider David to be someone he would trust with his confidences, he would, however, almost trust him with his life. There was an arrogance and a middle-class self-assurance in Michael, which David had found to be a few cuts above himself and therefore very alluring. That Michael was a 'snooty so and so', David had recognised and had often told him so.

Michael had persuaded his parents to let him rent a small terrace house which he could try to persuade a friend to share with him. Naturally he could not expect his friend to pay much towards the rental since this friend would be doing him a favour. So, with the help of the student liaison officer at the college, he had managed to find a two down three up property. His parents had followed him up with his things in a car while he rode on his bike.

There were two bedrooms of similar size at the front and back of the first floor, with a third smaller front box room across the landing from the bathroom. He had chosen the back room for himself so as to be away from the road, but also because it had a lock to it. Assuming that David was bound to have friends crawling all around the house, this would provide him with a degree of privacy.

He had provided the bedclothes for the two rooms and bought a used desk for the box room, making it into a study. There was already a double sofa in the front sitting room to which he had added two large bean bags. The dining room at the back had a small dining table with four chairs which were quite adequate for their use. He spent some time scrubbing and disinfecting the bathroom and kitchen and was quite pleased with what he had achieved. And in each room he made sure there was an ashtray. There were two blue pressed metal ashtrays promoting *Benskin's* beer in the house, to which he had added three glass ones.

He wanted the year to start well and was quite excited to know what David would think of the place. He could have had a two bedroom property, but they all appeared to have the front door opening directly into the sitting room. The present property, at one end of a terrace of four houses, benefited from a side passage with a wooden gate leading to the back garden where he could safely park his Yamaha.

On entering number 26, one is faced with a long hallway that ends with the door into the kitchen. To the left there is a long, straight staircase to the upper floor and on the right are the two doors to the two reception rooms which were left open. Glancing into them as he and Michael walked to the kitchen, David was astonished at how unlike a student dig the whole place was. To start with it was not malodorous as their last dig was. It intrigued and bothered him as to how much Michael was paying for the place, which he had offered to David at £18 a week. Surely that was extremely generous of him. Michael could have turned one of the reception rooms into another rental room. On the other hand, David knew how unhappy Michael was the previous year and could appreciate his wish to be rid of other lodgers.

It was beyond his comprehension why Michael had chosen him to be his housemate but, having spent ten days on holiday in France with him, he knew it would work out. He knew that they were the antithesis of the proverbial two peas in the pod, but genuine affection from Michael and the same affection and respect from him would make the arrangement a success. He was not without concern that his untidiness, the result of being looked after in every way at home, and his social circle of friends who were bound to visit, might annoy Michael. He was certain Michael must have taken that into consideration.

'What in the world have you got here, David?' Michael laughed as he brought out four cans of corned beef, two large baking potatoes, apples and oranges, cans of peas and baked beans, a bottle of tomato sauce and a small freezer bag containing bacon and sausages. 'And bloody onions!' he chuckled.

'It makes my mum happy to do this – no harm done,' David protested.

'No, not at all. I find it quite touching actually. They must spoil you rotten. Tell you what, we can have the spuds for dinner. I have some ham and cheese in the fridge. Let me show you your room and you can settle in while I cook.'

'Why didn't you take the double bed?' David asked as he was shown both the rooms.

'I don't fidget in bed,' Michael replied. 'A single's just as good for me. It gives me more room for a work desk. You can use the study – if study is something you do.'

'Study is something I do, Michael. Well, at least it is something I'll have to do – before long,' David happily admitted. He had reverted to using Michael's name, finding it somehow more appropriate.

Since getting to Watford, David had had little time to think of Gloria. Lying in bed now, with his eyes shut, he began to doze off as comforting images of her descended upon him like a soft, downy duvet inviting him to drift away to Gloria land. He had never touched a girl so soft, of curves so defined, and so responsive to every touch. Not a tall girl, but so complete and of such a sweet nature that they never had a harsh word for each other. Other girls had meant to him what girls were meant to be for boys – objects of powerful sexual interest and gratification until they fell in love. There had always been a coarseness about them which served the purpose well enough at the time.

Gloria was different. He liked her as a person first, when he saw her again in the summer after a lapse of two years when they were together at school. He had turned around from serving a customer when he recognised her. She was buying some apples and talking to his mother and he caught the tail end of their conversation. For the last two months she had been training as a hairdresser at the salon a little up the road. They had a little chat and a couple of weekends later they met up to see a show. It helped too that his mother actually liked her. So Gloria became a fixture of his summer vacation. And then there was Michael and France.

It had been a long, tiring day on the underground and changing stations across London with his heavy bags. Although the room was new to him, the fact that Michael was there prevented him from feeling strange, and he was fast asleep by the time Michael called up to him.

Not getting an answer from David, Michael went upstairs to see what was going on.

'Jesus wept!' he exclaimed, chuckling to himself, to see that David had so quickly fallen asleep, all curled up like a wild cub in its lair, softly but surely snoring. Michael decided to leave the potatoes till later and went across to his room to connect up a turntable and speakers.

He had brought with him a stack of LPs of classical music – Beethoven, Rachmaninov, Liszt, Erik Satie and Rimsky among them, but his taste in music was eclectic. On a separate stack were albums of Roxy Music, the Eagles, Pink Floyd, the Who, the Beatles, Fleetwood Mac and Donna Summer. He believed that where music and books were concerned, it was to each his own. Whether it was classical music, jazz, rock or sentimental ballads, as long as one was discerning within the genre, one was justified in enjoying it.

He hated the snobbery displayed by his parents with regards to music. His mother was a piano teacher and sang with *the London Philharmonic chorus*. While being an accountant professionally, his father also played the clarinet for a London orchestra. No music was proper music unless it was classical. In Michael's view that was like saying no book was a proper book unless it were a Shakespeare or a Dickens.

It was inevitable that he would grow to love classical music because from an early age he was exposed to it and was taught how to play the piano. However, he embraced pop music as a teenager like any other boy would. As he grew older, he discovered jazz and Sinatra and Spanish guitars. He learned pretty soon not to have to justify his taste in music. In a gentle rebelliousness to his parent's bigoted attitude, he learned to play the 'common' guitar.

After setting up the turntable, the first record he chose to play that afternoon was *Barbra Streisand – first album*, which he had bought at a charity shop. He loved the freshness and crispness of this early recording with its foreboding rendition of *Cry Me a River* and its rousing and gutsy belter of *Happy Days Are Here Again*. In particular, he was fond of the *A Taste of Honey* track. He lay in bed, relaxed, letting the music surround him, realizing that he was not being his parents' son in more ways than in this. 'A profession, Michael, is what you should aim for,' rang in his ears. Becoming a doctor or an engineer or a lawyer was what his parents had envisaged for his future. Beyond those spheres they could not grasp.

It was precisely because of his own family background that Michael had turned sceptical about the professions. He had countless aunts and uncles, cousins and then cousins, who were doctors or lawyers or engineers and in his father's case a chartered accountant. All decent people, he knew, and high achievers. But a few of them could bore the world for

Britain! Besides, for all their success and academic achievement, they had not engendered any passion in him.

For the past few years, Michael had come to the conclusion that being brilliant in a profession, despite the concentration of knowledge and the experience of execution, did not equate being intellectual or being liberal. These people were tied down too much, too tunnelled in their vision, by the discipline of their trade. He, on the other hand, needed more room to breathe. He was excellent academically, but he was not willing to sacrifice his life to a profession. Although aware of his own limitation in all directions he could envisage, he still wanted an occupation which was not so self-absorbed that it could not leave his mind free to love or to wallow where he pleased.

David raised his wrist to his face and started with a sinking feeling to find that it was almost 7 o'clock. Hardly refreshed by his sleep, he felt guilty that he had left Michael on his own to get on with the preparation of dinner, which should have been ready some while ago. He could smell the baked potatoes and was suddenly hungry and went sheepishly down to the kitchen.

'Sorry, Michael, I just dropped off.'

'That's OK.' Michael laughed, 'you still look exhausted.'

'It's travelling through London, and I'd a late night last night with Gloria.'

'It's tough leaving her behind, I guess,' Michael added. 'Spuds would be ready in 30 minutes.'

'I'll have a quick shower then.'

It occurred to Michael that in the previous spring David was also in love, but the fact that this time round he was not garrulous about it suggested to him that it might be of a more serious nature. Some people need someone in their life at all time, he observed, with an incredulous shake of his head. David had a very quick shower and then asked if he could run to make a quick call to Gloria. It reminded Michael to chase up his application for the telephone.

'Go towards St John's Road and take a left turn and there's a phone box there,' Michael said, '- about 50 yards.'

Twenty minutes later, he returned, with a bashful look on his face, embarrassed by his own devotion to Gloria. Michael pretended not to notice and, throughout the meal, the subject of Gloria did not arise. They decided that they would go into town later to meet up with friends who might have got back for the new term.

'Jorge's back from Caracas,' Michael mentioned,' I saw him at the *Coach Maker* last night. Craig Paley, Natalie, Dickie and Kirsty were all there.'

'Was Clinger there?' asked David.

'Clingier than ever,' was Michael's tongue in cheek reply.

At five foot one, squat of build, with an attractive round face constantly embellished with a smile, Janet

Granger, referred to by many as Clinger because of the way she would hold on to a male friend's sleeve, was an amiable character, generally liked by all. Over the previous year she had taken a liking to Michael and they sometimes made quite an odd looking pair, although no one took them to be a couple. Dressed usually in blue jeans and a loosely knitted woollen jumper, she contrasted sharply with Michael's ability to carry off whatever clothes he wore. With his usual self-assurance, Michael had not taken offence at Clinger but had treated her like a little sister.

She was at the *Coach Maker* together with dozens of other students from the college. Michael picked her up and gave her a twirl, followed by David who did the same – all to Clinger's delighted laughter.

'Beware of these guys!' exclaimed, Dickie.

'I shall be most careful, Dickie,' she laughed.

The conversation turned to football, the wonderful summer, who had done what, a little about the new term at College, when they could get together for a game of squash, and who was going to get the next round.

David was in his element. Michael observed how quickly David could absorb and expand at the same time into his immediate surrounding. There was not a thought in any direction beyond that sphere he was in. Standing among them, with Clinger by his side, Michael was with them and yet not a part of the loudness and the general conversation. Occasionally someone would turn to him and say something to him personally and they would talk for a little. Or someone else might pull him slightly aside to ask him about his Yamaha or about college work. He was quite comfortable with his role in the situation and enjoyed watching David having a good time.

Leaning against the bar, he had a 180 degree view of the room, and he noticed Lars, a second year Norwegian student, quietly chatting to a lady he had not seen before. She looked different – older than the other girls at college. He wondered who she was.

He liked the warm glow cast by the lights through veils of smoke upon faces in a pub. It transported him straightaway from the uncertain world outside into a paradigm of anticipated behaviours, of laughter, of jests, of slight flirtations on the part of the intrusive young, and of looks of disapproval, of grimness and of world weariness on the part of the older locals. To him it appeared like an old oil painting with a honeyed veneer that bound together the shadows and the highlights of diverse images, making them an entity. Within that entity, there was a place for him just as there was a place for David or that lady with the dark brown hair, with a cigarette in her hand.

Rodger Wilder moved over to Michael and suggested a game of squash on the Wednesday after class. He was an all-round sportsman from South Africa and although Michael was nowhere close to his standard at squash, he had enjoyed the few games they had together. Clinger asked if she could come along and watch, to which Rodger said, 'You should come along and play!'

'Come on now, Rodge,' she retorted, 'can you imagine me with a racquet?'

A burst of robust laughter distracted them. David was demonstrating his experience with eating an oyster with his left index finger and thumb pinching his nose and with the other index finger and thumb holding an imaginary oyster towards his mouth and making a glurp, glurp sound at the same time. Lars and his friend turned towards them and, after saying something to her, he stood up and brought her to the group.

'Hi, you're having fun!' he said to his boisterous college mates and, turning towards her, he introduced his friend as Jacqueline. Michael could not make out the conversation that went on because Rodger and Clinger were talking to him and, in the din of the pub, Bryan Ferry was blaring down about *These Foolish Things*. Soon after, Jorge suggested that they should all drink up and go to *Baileys*, a night club on the first floor over shops on The Parade. A little known group called *'Blue Timing'* was performing there, it seemed. David walked over and asked if they should go.

'You go along,' Michael replied, 'I have some work to do.'

David did not push him, knowing that it was not his scene.

'Oh, come on, Michael, please come,' pleaded Clinger to no avail.

'David will be there – that's more than enough company for you, Clinger. Who knows, it might be your lucky night.'

'Well, it might be your lucky night too. Do come!' exclaimed Clinger.

'I think it is already my lucky night, Clinger,' Michael said.

'Oh, do tell. What is it that we don't know?'

'That would be telling,' Michael replied teasingly and then laughed. 'Go along and have a good time.'

Besides Michael, everyone else was going except for Jacqueline. Lars suggested he took her back to the YMCA[1] before joining the group, but Jacqueline was insistent that she would be quite alright walking back by herself. Michael said that the YM was on his way home, so he would be delighted to accompany her. It was another quarter of an hour before the group left for *Bailey*s. Michael and Jacqueline stayed back to finish their drinks.

Jacqueline stopped just outside the *Coach Maker* and offered Michael a cigarette, which he refused. He apologised for not having a lighter or matches to light it for her. She took out a gold fluted lighter from her bag and, cupping the cigarette from the breeze, lit it. In spite of the smoke from the cigarette, Michael could discern a light perfume from her, which he had not noticed before. It was there for a moment and then it was gone.

---

[1] The old redbrick YMCA at Clarendon Road

'Don't you like dancing?' Michael asked as they walked.

'You mean why have I not joined the others? Of course I love dancing and I have had my fair share of it in the last few years. How shall I put it? I am not a good dancer. I would dance among complete strangers or among friends. But I would have felt uncomfortable among your friends whom I have just met. Give me time, Michael, and I might make a fool of myself yet. But you, you should be with them.'

'Unlike you, I actually cannot dance. You won't find anyone more clumsy or uncoordinated than I am.'

Pausing to look at Michael, Jacqueline commented, 'I would have thought you would be a good mover.'

'Then you are much mistaken, Jacqueline,' Michael laughed. 'Do you know Watford at all, or is it new to you?'

'Not just Watford, but everything is new to me here. The YM, the people I have met, the new life – all interesting to me, and I have only been here five days. Now it is your turn to fill me in.'

'I'm in my second year doing Print. David, whom you had met earlier, and I share a house towards Watford Junction[1]. We are on the same Printing course. Which course are you taking?'

'Advertising Admin – a one year course. I have little idea what it would entail, but it should be interesting. I like the idea of having a year planned for me. No

---

[1] Main Railway Station at Watford

urgent decisions to make. What about you? I presume you are not local since you are house sharing.'

'Oh no, I am from St. Albans – not that far from here though. And you?'

'I'm from Reading.'

They soon reached the YMCA on Clarendon Road. Just before they did so, Jacqueline lit another cigarette and there was again that faint scent which flickered and dimmed and took Michael by surprise once more.

'Well, thank you for walking me back. I presume it is inevitable that we would bump into each other again.'

'Certainly. This is a small town and we students tend to be everywhere. Besides, David and I normally walk past the YM on our way to and from College. You can't get away from me that easily, you know.'

'Who said I was trying to?' she smiled archly. 'Goodnight.'

It was past 10 o'clock, but it was still warm and the sky was unusually clear and light for the time of the year. Michael walked home with an unaccustomed lightness of head and of steps, not knowing why, but feeling in his heart an acknowledgement of having been intrigued in a way he was yet to understand. He went up to his room and put on a light leather jacket, deciding to go for a ride on his Yamaha. It occurred to him that he had forgotten to give a set of house keys to David, but he did not expect him back till the early hours of the morning. He got onto St. Albans Road and rode out of Watford towards the countryside. On his mind was a niggling awareness that he had to be back before David.

Mr Sumner was the lecturer in Philosophy. A bespectacled man in his early fifties, of medium height, slightly portly, he was kindly and always wore a bemused smile. To whatever proposition a student came up with he would smile and suggest another way of looking at the situation. 'What is' and 'what isn't' could often be coloured by what one thinks 'it is'. He insisted one should first discover what one thinks 'it is' then remove what is irrelevantly subjective to derive at the objective truth. However, he believed that so much of humanity is based on subjective interactions that we must always be conscious of its existence. He would then chuckle and say, 'but I might be wrong!'

It had been some years since Jacqueline had had the opportunity to talk seriously with someone older and wiser than she. She had remained behind in the class to debate a point with him on where the responsibility lay with personal choices in an age where the media intruded into every aspect of one's life. Was it a personal choice when one's decision was guided and channelled and funnelled into the making of it? On the other hand, different people did respond differently to the same set of manipulative external influences. Did that not indicate that it was the person rather than the external factors which pre-destined a decision?

Why then, Mr Sumner threw back at her, did she think advertisers targeted their readers and audience?

Could that be because they knew how certain target groups might respond in a certain way, taking into account their socio-economic background, their particular family pattern, their educational attainment, their cultural experience? Was that not an attempt at engineering a decision?

For the first time someone had actively elicited her points of view, had listened to them and had even invited dissent. She found that exciting. Whether it had been with Gérard or Edward, it had always been a situation of listening and learning and silent questioning.

They had been the experienced ones, the confident ones and in a passively chauvinistic way had held control over her development as a person. Neither had asked for her views. Each had told her what their views were. She had no doubt that if she had questioned more, had put forward more reasoned arguments, Edward would have welcome it and their relationship might have been even more valuable. But who was she to have considered her views worth presenting? Although in many ways she felt she had been manipulated, there was no misgiving about her past. However, she was eagerly grateful now to be independent and be self-assured for the first time. Instead of being wary of what was new, she was ready to face, accept, confront and manage whatever might come her way.

'Please forgive me,' Edward had pleaded. It came out as a wispy, tender, dry whisper, which was all that his strength could summon.

'Forgive you?' Jacqueline had asked in bewilderment. 'Why, I owe all these years to you, Edward. I do not know how I could have survived so sanely if it were not for you,' she said. 'All the books and poetry you had introduced to me, all the advice and knowledge you had provided would cushion me through the rest of my life. Edward, I feel I have inherited a treasure trove from you'

'You do not need a cushion, Jacqueline. Cushions are for the old and infirm who have nothing left to look forward to. And age would descend and surprise you sooner than you might expect. The weight of it, Jacqueline, the weight of it when it comes. You need to go out there now and discover your own treasure troves. Do not stay back here. Go out into the world. It's all my fault. I should have made you go long ago. Gérard was never going to come back. I knew. You are young. There's money. Do not remain behind. I was selfish, you see. I needed you – like a daughter I never had. Someone to talk to. Someone to be close to. It's not too late. Go.'

He clasped her hand and she could see the pain in his eyes even though there were no tears. 'Gérard – it's been over, Jacqueline. You must go and see him. Get a resolution on the situation and then move on.'

'Are you sure you do not want me to call Nigel?' she digressed.

'He would not come. Do not bother him. Ever since I left their mother, they had not forgiven me – Nigel and Colin,' he explained. He closed his eyes and after a few minutes he opened them and looked tiredly at Jacqueline. 'You are here.'

Three weeks later, just after the Easter break, Edward had died peacefully in the middle of the night. It was not till the following spring that Jacqueline had picked herself up and rang Rod Payne, an old colleague of Gérard's in Reading. She arranged to meet him at the *Caversham Bridge Hotel*[1] just south of the Thames. Jacqueline had only met Rod four or five times while Gérard was in Reading and had liked him, but he remained, as it should be, Gérard's friend. The last thing she wanted was to put him in a difficult position, which, by the awkwardness she perceived in him when they met, was what she suspected she had done. He had wondered what it was she was after, over 4 years after Gérard had left.

She cheerfully rectified the situation by getting to the point, which immediately put Rod at ease. Of the many things she had learned from Gérard, one stood out. A man cannot cope with an emotional woman unless all that emotion is centred on him and even then only when he is desirous of it. In spite of many years of marriage and being the father of 4 children, Rod was not normally comfortable in the company of women.

---

[1] The Hotel no longer exists being replaced by a much larger one.

He considered Jacqueline as an acquaintance rather than as a friend. His friend was Gérard and he would resent Jacqueline inveigling any information from him which might be detrimental to Gérard.

What came to pass was somewhat more innocuous. Jacqueline had simply asked him to pass on a letter to Gérard and to let him know that she was well – all quite proper and above board. In the letter she had requested that they met up. She had a few questions that needed answers to, and then they could part as friends. It was not till November that she received a reply suggesting that they met up at Düsseldorf in January. He would be there for a business conference for a few days. It was a long time to January for someone who was holding back her life, but for Gérard, who had already got on with his, there did not appear to be any urgency.

The cold blue and green neon signs of *Die Signallampe* [1] hotel flashed through the thin, beige curtain, casting faint shifting shadows of the wall lamps and the furniture. The small radiator below the window gurgled with trapped air but emitted little heat. Through the double glazed window the muffled sounds of trains and station announcements just a few hundred metres away filtered in like uneasy distant reminders that there was a world outside, and that that world was complex, made up of thousands of

---

[1] The Signal Lamp

individuals like herself, each with his own joy or sorrow, with his own expectation or disappointment.

Jacqueline paced the floor. She looked out of the window into the drab, grey winter afternoon. She lay in bed with a book. Feeling uneasy at heart, she got up again and sat in the chair. Had anything untoward happened to him? Surely he would not let her down? Perhaps she had given him the incorrect information? By the following afternoon, she knew decidedly that he would not come.

She held her pain tightly within her, denying it access to overwhelm her. Hunger suddenly jolted her. She put on an extra jumper and her overcoat and walked defiantly in the bitterly cold afternoon to the Hauptbanhof[1] and bought a bratwurst in a roll. She took the first turning into Graf-Adolf-Strasse and just trudged on until she came to the bridge that straddled the canal that ran between the East and West sides of Königsallee. The lightest, finest, snow began to fall. She somehow made her way to the Altstadt[2] and wandered from narrow street to narrow street, half expecting that she would run into him.

When she reached the bank of the Rhine it was already dark and huge flakes of snow weighed down from above. She could just about make out the hazy amber lights from the other bank. How immense was nature, she thought. How incomprehensible was

---

[1] Central Station
[2] Old Town

nature. Yet what value had nature but for man's perception of it? What value had it if she had not witnessed it, that her mood had not been modified by it, that she had not shivered in it? Ultimately it was the immensity and incomprehensibility of mankind that existed supreme. She was important. Her pain was important. Her future in whatever form was important.

Everyone's life must be paramount to himself. Gérard had the right to choose to be free from her. No one was responsible for our sanity or happiness. She had to learn to be strong. How could she be strong against a world she had so little experience of?

When she returned to the hotel, she decided that she would stay for a few more days in Düsseldorf. There were no reasons to hurry back to England. She was exhausted and damp. Above all she was confused. There was unexplained guilt, there was anger, and there was emptiness in her heart. She had to sort her life out. She would sort things out.

Edward used to encourage her to write down her feelings. 'We can't all write well, but what does it matter? It is a platform from which we can see the pattern of our emotions and our thoughts. It is a distancing of what is volatile within us into the concrete. It can help us to see more clearly the truth or absurdity of our state of mind.' She picked up her pen and wrote onto a note book about the queer sensation of confusion mingled with loss, but of what loss she was uncertain.

Did you find me then?
Who had lost his way?
Through which twisting,
Steamy alley,
Down which stairs?
Through which door,
Rusted, exfoliating,
Did you hear me sigh?
Did I call out?
Did I let you go?
Where was I?

'Sorry to keep you waiting, Frank,' Neal, the Marketing lecturer, apologised.

'That's alright. Jacqueline here has been keeping me excellent company,' Mr Sumner replied.

'Hi, Neal,' Jacqueline greeted Mr Norman. She was still not used to calling the lecturers by their first name, but felt it was sensible to go along with how it was at college.

'Sorry! I had interrupted you.'

'No, not at all,' Jacqueline exclaimed, 'I was just about to go up to the canteen,' and she thanked Frank for his time and went briskly up the stairs.

Most of the students had already left the canteen by the time Jacqueline got there. With only 15 minutes left before the next class, she decided to have just a coffee and an apple crumble. Walking across to Michael, who was on his own, she asked if she might join him. Although she had seen him with David from a distance a few times, she had not met him again since they walked to the YMCA together a couple of weeks ago.

'Where is your friend?'

'Who? David? He's gone into town with a few friends. We are not conjoined twins, you know. Really!' Michael laughed. 'How are you finding things here?' he enquired.

'Marvellous. I love being with other students and the lecturers are friendly and great to talk to.'

'You talk to the lecturers outside of class?' Michael teased.

'Selectively.'

'Still enjoying life at Watford?' Michael added.

'How much time have you, Michael? I'm loving it.'

'Certainly not much time today, but how would you like to come with me on my bike this Saturday? We could get out of Watford and have lunch somewhere.'

Did her eyes, fleetingly, betray a twinkle of amusement? Was she laughing at him? Had he been summarily dismissed as inadequate? He looked up enquiringly.

'It's the best offer I've had yet. I'd love that,' she accepted, drinking up her coffee. After making arrangement for Michael to pick her up at the YMCA, she rose and left, leaving Michael, standing, amazed at the serendipitous outcome.

It couldn't have been better if he had planned it. He had no idea where he would take her, but there were still 2 days for him to think about it. David would be back at home at Uxbridge at the weekend as usual, and there was no reason to mention it and open himself to questioning. It was simply an arrangement to go on an outing. Yet, why was he rationalising and, in a disquieting way, explaining away the significance of this triumph? And could it be considered as a triumph when there had been no prior intent?

He busied himself in the early evening cleaning the Yamaha and polishing it with the usual care and deliberation that he would normally lend to a task. He dusted the crash helmet that Jacqueline was to use and placed it safe alongside his on the desk in the bedroom. He had bought it second hand a year ago when Clinger and Angelina, an insistent Nigerian girl, had asked to be taken on a ride, and it had recently been kept in the small garden shed at the end of the garden.

David had gone to the pub without him. He had often allowed David to coax him into going to town but, on this occasion, he wished to avoid running into Jacqueline. He would spend the evening reading and listening to music. However, that did not prove to be easy. He was uncertain of what he had done at the spur of the moment. It was not unusual for him to invite someone to go for a ride on his bike, but the fact that this thought had shadowed him the remaining of the day had troubled him.

He did not know Jacqueline. The night he first saw her at the pub something had stirred in him. He was enchanted by the way the light had cast a honeyed glow on her with soft shadows that shifted as she spoke and moved her slender arm as she drew the cigarette towards her lips. Then when he walked her back, he thought there was a slight rapport between them and could not help smiling afterwards at the subtle teasing in her voice. Normally he was very much in control of situations, not allowing his feelings to be drawn, aloof and judgmental. But that night he felt that it was he who was being judged, that it was he who was being toyed with. He didn't dislike it.

On Friday evening he walked David to Watford Junction. After saying goodbye, he went back to the house, feeling a little listless as he usually did when David had gone back home. There was a little cheese left in the fridge and he made himself a sandwich and, as the weather was rather close, he sat in the back garden, listening to his Sony transistor radio. He resisted from going to the pub but, at 8 o'clock, Clinger rang and asked if he could give her a lift and join her at a house warming party at King's Langley. Some chap she got to know at the Bingo Hall, where she worked 2 nights a week, had bought a small terrace property there. Anticipating a long, anxious night ahead of him, he was quite happy for a diversion. Besides, he always enjoyed Clinger's company.

The party was at full swing by the time they got there, but they were in time for the tail end of the barbecue. The 15 or so people there formed quite a noisy crowd. Michael was glad that he knew nobody. He would rather be among strangers, especially those he was unlikely to meet again, than to be among acquaintances he had to strike up conversation with.

By the time he dropped Clinger home and got back, it was past mid-night. The air was still uncomfortably heavy and humid. He quickly stripped and, after the initial shock, relaxed and enjoyed the cool shower.

A rumble of thunder woke him up at 4 o'clock. He peeped out of the window and to his dismay, it was drizzling. All hot summer long it had been dry and just when it could have served a purpose, it gave in to the rain. By daybreak, however, the rain had ceased and a light, lifting mist promised another bright September day. Michael checked the spare helmet to make sure it was clean after the previous evening's use. He lifted the wet plastic sheet that covered his Yamaha and wiped the bike with a hand-towel in case any moisture was trapped on it. He then had some cereals and a cup of coffee and was ready to venture out. Everything felt normal. He hoped it would be a fun day but did not wish to anticipate.

'Is there any place you would like to see?' he asked Jacqueline.

'I'm all yours,' she smiled. 'This area is all fresh to me. I'm a Berkshire Oxfordshire person.' She tucked her hair under the crash helmet and zipped up her light, olive coloured leather jacket.

'What are you laughing at?'

'I'm afraid the helmet looks rather large on you. Are you comfortable?' he enquired.

'It's OK once it's strapped up. We are not letting little details spoil our day, are we?'

They headed off towards Rickmansworth and from there, taking the minor roads, they came close to Chalfont St Giles and then Amersham. Riding through woodlands, he gathered speed a little and she held on to his waist. Many a woman had done that before but this time he automatically, though only momentarily, straightened his back, strangely aware of the definite pressure on him. It was a simple sensation, so ephemeral that he had to try hard to re-capture it late into that night.

The woodlands they passed were rather sombre. The leaves had only just begun to turn. He decided to ride around Hemel Hempstead and turned towards St Albans on the Verulam Road. Being familiar with the town, he soon found a place to leave his bike and they walked along St Peter's Street towards the town. His heart swelled with pleasure at the joy in Jacqueline's face as she discovered the Saturday market.

Up St Peter's Street towards Chequer Street and Market Place, the vibrant market stalls stretched on both sides. She was fascinated with the size and the variety of completely unrelated goods on sales side by side. It reminded her of markets she knew in France. Towels, trinkets, crafts, lampshades, fruit and veg, little glass ornaments – she delighted in them all. She put a pair of huge gold plated earrings against her ears and laughed at the horror she saw on Michael's face. Finally she settled for a pair of small hand crafted enamel earrings – with Michael's approval.

Towards Market Place they stopped at a stall selling prints. Michael chose one of the *Abbey Cathedral* in watercolour for Jacqueline. She thanked him with a kiss on the cheek and in return got him a print of Degas' *Rehearsal of a Ballet on Stage*.

'I don't think I can make myself eat it, but doesn't that burger smell wonderful! All that caramelised onions!' she remarked.

'Let's get something to eat,' he suggested and they hurried to a pub further up the street.

'What would you like?'

'Oh, the beef and Guinness pie please,' she replied. 'Sounds delicious!'

'I think I'll have the same.'

'Shall we have some chips too?'

'You know, I am really having such a good time. I feel the joy of youth. That's what going to College, living at the YM and being out with you today have made me feel. I don't think I was ever young. I was a child and then I was a kept woman,' she said and laughed. 'Have I shocked you, Michael?'

'I don't think so. From the first time I saw you, from the way you talked and moved, I told myself – here's a kept woman if ever there was one,' he beamed at her.

'A kept woman who has never been young. Doesn't it scare you a little, Michael, to be with a woman who has lived? Who has a past – several Pasts?' she mused, stressing the word 'lived'.

'I am fearless, Jacqueline,' he joked. 'And I am fascinated,' he added in a softened tone.

It occurred to him that in his case it was a childhood that was missing. Whenever he saw children around him, carefree, bold, free to express themselves, there rose within him a tinge of envy and bitterness.

He grew up within the framework of a formula of good behaviour, be seen and not heard, be sensible, be talented, be clean. It was like young bones being set so that whatever later development there might be, they could never quite set themselves free of their acquired structure. In a way he exuded confidence. He had the facility of learned responses. Socially he was at ease, though rather reticent. But when it came to direct emotional involvement, he was less adept. He had a wit about him, but he was never quite free to embroil himself carelessly with people.

'Here comes the dour waitress with the pies,' Michael said.

'Or have the pies come with the dour waitress?' Jacqueline laughed.

The pies sat in their individual earthenware dish, each placed to one side of copious amount of sad, overcooked carrots and peas on a white plate. Then the chips arrived in a large bowl. Michael and Jacqueline looked at each other.

'The pie smells delicious,' Jacqueline commented. 'In France they don't often serve much vegetable with their main course. At times one wonders if that might be a good thing.'

'The crust is not bad,' Michael said.

They looked at each other and burst out laughing.

'What's that mush in there? It does smell good though,' Jacqueline observed.

'Would you like to order something else instead?'

'No, no. We can have the chips and, as you said, the crust isn't that bad.'

They ate what they could but, for dessert, they left and bought 2 double scoop ice cream from the market. At the top of Market Place they crossed the High Street into a narrow alley and then through the East Gate into the Abbey Cathedral Garden. They sat on the grass and as the sun was still strong, they lay on it when they had finished the ice cream.

'Jacqueline?'

'Hmm?'

'How would you like to be called? Jacqui, Jacque, Jacqueline?'

'It does not make any difference to me, really. When I was young, my parents and all my friends called me Jacqui. But I'm used to Jacqueline now.'

'How's that?'

'A long time ago, Gérard, my then partner, insisted that I called myself Jacqueline. I'd left a note for him when I went out one day – quite early in our relationship. I'd signed it Jacqui. He was ridiculously livid when I got back. He was very particular about details. Things had to be done in a certain way. There were always reasons for them so one did not argue. Jamais, jamais ne t'appelles toi Jacqui, he shouted. Jacqueline, n'est-ce pas un assez bon nom ? Pourquoi voudras tu le detruire? [1] I must admit it sounds better said the French way with the more rounded "a" sound.' But one didn't argue then. You know Michael, he wouldn't get away with that now.

'How long were you with him?'

'Oh, a long time. About 12 years.'

'Was he good to you?'

'You ask a lot of questions.'

'Do you mind?'

'No. Not really. You are young and you are curious,' she said, but did not give him an answer to his question.

'So what have you found so interesting about Watford?'

'Not specifically about Watford, but just being at College and at the YM. You see, for the first time in my life I feel free from having to prove to myself that I am free. The last 3 years, travelling and living in Germany and France, I was trying to make up for lost time, being reckless, getting hurt, misunderstanding situations. Here, I'm more of an observer, understanding and seeing myself through other people as a foil,' she said, turning sideway to look at Michael.

She was surprised to notice what a lovely dark chocolate colour his hair was. She had always taken it to be very dark but, in the sun, it had acquired a richer tone to it. She rose, followed by Michael.

---

[1] Never, never call yourself Jacqui. Isn't Jacqueline a good enough name? Why would you wish to destroy it?

'Hold on,' she said, picking a few blades of dry grass from Michael's hair and shirt, and turning around for him to reciprocate. They walked leisurely towards the Cathedral while she talked of the people she had got to know at the YMCA. Before they went into the Cathedral, he pointed out St Albans Boy's School just across the lane from the Cathedral, where he had spent 4 years. He was not forthcoming about his days there and Jacqueline knew better than to try to elicit information from someone who seemed to hold so much to his chest.

The market at Place Courtonne by the Bassin Saint Pierre was in full swing. The Bar of the *Hotel L'Univers* was crowded both inside and on the terrace. Marking time with a large cup of breakfast coffee, Jacqueline sat watching the ever disarranging crowd at the Sunday morning market at Caen. She felt invigorated by the aroma of coffee around her and the smell of bread and of chicken and pork being roasted on rotisseries from within the market.

It had been almost three years since that long, lonely, agonising wait at *Die Signallampe* hotel. She had spent very little of that time in England, treading as on a stage through Düsseldorf, Cologne and Hamburg before ending up in the South of France – through Jimmy Fogg, an American saxophonist with cherry red patent shoes, to Hans, a bogus industrialist-writer, who worked at the dock at Hamburg, to Mario, an aspiring artist at Aix-en Provence, whose provenance led to a small fishing port near Marseilles. She had heard the music and danced to the songs. The joints had been lit, the glass had been jauntily clinked, the smile had been fixed, the lights had been dimmed, the eyes were arid and the fear had gone.

Gérard had finally written to ask if she would like to go over to Caen for a few days while his wife and children were on a visit to her family at Montgiroux. It was a short and casual letter without any emotional content. Jacqueline had smiled to herself at its wisdom. Perhaps it was time they got together and sorted out their unfinished business.

When he left England, there were no promises made that he would return nor was there a final severance. The years since had been a long, unwieldy, unpunctuated passage of time. Jacqueline felt that had she seen Gérard at Düsseldorf, she might not have dealt with the situation with the maturity and good sense that she now possessed. She ordered another coffee and looked at her watch. It was early yet but, having arrived very early, she felt she had been waiting a long time.

From between a stall selling lady's clothes and another selling locally produced vegetables, Gérard had finally seen her. He could not recognise her at first, so much had she changed. Initially, he felt disappointed with rising resentment to find so little vestige of the woman he had so carefully constructed.

He had primed her to be a woman comme il faut[1], neat and subtle, dressed with chic and simplicity – never loud in appearance or in speech.

He and his wife, Fleur, had grown up together and married young. He had always accepted her as she was. He saw Jacqueline differently. Jacqueline was slender, tall and young – so malleable in form and in spirit. And what was this apparition sitting outside the bar?

He noticed first her hair. It was the hair that had made him scan past her earlier – past a flower stall on one side and a low vegetable stall on the other. Instead of the beautiful, rich brown hair, smooth and straight, he beheld a short crop, tinted, glaringly so, in an orangey blonde. The short hair gave an angularity to her face far from the softly defined features he used to like. Her lips were a wide gash of dark, orangey red. It was almost a parody of a Lautrec music hall dancer – and in daylight too. She wore a faded khaki T-shirt which hung loosely over her faded blue jeans.

Here was, he decided, a young woman who had belatedly found her freedom to experiment and to grow up, quite inappropriately. Then he thought, she was so far from the Jacqueline he knew that it might make it easier to sit down and talk, easier to get up and go.

'Jacqueline.'

'Gérard, Ça va?'[1]

---

[1] As a woman ought to be

'Oui, je vais bien, et tois?[2]' he asked, studying her face.

She offered him a cigarette in case he still smoked. He refused it. She lit her cigarette, smiled and looked back at him. She felt more comfortable than she had anticipated. They had gone their separate ways and it no longer mattered what he thought of her. She wanted to study him, as a grown, experienced woman would study him. Had she really loved him? Why on earth stayed so many years with someone if she had not really loved him? More importantly, had he ever loved her? She did not have to question him. She felt that she would know just by being with him again.

In a strange way he had not changed. A little older, a little greyer, but still the charming, self-assertive man he had always been. She felt a little sad that in a way he had come across as of another generation. It was as if she had learned to be young and he had been left behind.

Was it the case, she asked herself, that people with the strongest convictions were also the people who would be dated the soonest? Was it the case that theorists, bathed in the glory of their discoveries, would be the first to be eclipsed by the burst of other glorious ideas, unless they could adjust and accommodate? Somehow she felt that Gérard was

---

[1] Gérard, are you OK?
[2] Yes, I'm OK and you?

comfortable within him, but would, as years went by, find more and more to gripe about the changing world.

She had wanted to make sure that he was healthy and happy and with that she had not been disappointed. She had wanted to know if he had loved her when they were together. Perhaps in his own way he had, she thought. Shamefacedly, she had to admit that perhaps she was just a convenience while it lasted.

There was nothing in Gérard then that would make her ache for him. She had no longer any present need for him. But her pride had taken a battering. Which woman would not like to think that she had been loved and madly so? Which woman would not like to have possessed a man's soul even more than of his body?

> Ses bras – je ne les touche pas –
> Ils sont là.
> Le sourire qui vient, qui va,
> On ne se demande pas –
> Pourquoi ?
> On ne demande pas
> Sa sainteté –
> Comment pourrait-on ?
> On ne demande que son esprit,
> Complètement, son âme,
> Son amitié.[1]

---

[1] Un Moment en l'Été – see acknowledgements:
His arms – I didn't touch them – they were there. The smile which comes and goes, I didn't ask why. I ask not for his sanctity,

She wrote in her little book that night. It filled her with remorse that she had not been a cleverer person, one who could have manipulated him even better than he had manipulated her.

Gérard suggested that they drove to Cabourg for lunch. She would have loved to buy a rack of ribs from the rotisserie at the market, find a bench somewhere and dig into it. But she knew that that would be anathema to Gérard, so she conceded and they drove to Cabourg and lunched at a seaside restaurant.

He had the radio on in the car and hummed to the music, but once they had started enquiring about each other, the conversation flowed comfortably. She asked about his children, what they were doing, about his wife, about his work. He, in turn, wanted to know what she had been doing during the last few years. She told him about her stay in Germany, what she liked about the life there and how she had drifted to and through France and ended up at Aix-en-Provence before returning to England recently.

They could have been two people who had just met, sizing up each other, except that they each had a mental boundary of where the conversation must not go. They edged around all emotional issues. He was afraid of being drawn into a position of guilt. She was keen not to make him feel guilty or sorry for her.

---

how could I? I only ask for his spirit, completely for his soul, his friendship

To Gérard, their life together in England was an episode. It was an inevitable incident. If he had not been with her, he would have been with someone else. She was that reserved yet charming sketch of a girl he could add finishing touches to. A man abroad had need of a woman and she was that woman. Of course he had loved her. He was proud of her. But life had to go on and when he had to go back to France, it was the sensible thing to try and make a life with his estranged wife and family again. He had felt no guilt leaving Jacqueline. It was an affair that had come to its natural end. It was *pas grand-chose*[1].

He had treated her fairly. Although he had not given her any forwarding address or contact telephone number, he had rung her up every few weeks and had sent her money regularly to help with the rent until she had inherited a large fortune from her mother a couple of years later. That was an opportunity for him to break their contact.

The guilt that Gérard felt was for not turning up at the *Signallampe* hotel. It was cowardly of him. He was afraid that he might be weak and allow himself to get physically and emotionally involved while he was with her. Then, when he were to walk away again, that would be unfair to Jacqueline. To give false hope – that he would not do. He was aware of the hurt that he would have caused, but it was the best arrangement, he decided. Because it was Jacqueline who had asked for

---

[1] Nothing much (no big deal)

the meeting, he was afraid of a display of unreasoned female emotions.

This meeting at Caen was different. He had initiated it, calmly and sensibly as a man was wont to do. He wanted to make up for Düsseldorf. Jacqueline would have had plenty of time to gauge his position and understand that there would not be a future for them. He was taken aback at how casual Jacqueline had been. Although she had outwardly become this modern clash of bad taste, he found her new confidence and certitude of opinions quite arresting. There was a new person before him, in look and in character – someone so unexpectedly different that she had become interesting. He would not have minded if they could have met up every few months. He suddenly felt disadvantaged by this unexpected inclination.

When he tried to apologise and explain why he had not turned up in Düsseldorf, Jacqueline raised her hand and stopped him.

'Non, non, s'il te plait, Gérard. Ce n'est pas nécessaire. Tu as tes raisons, je le sais. Je le comprends.[1] The past is the past. You have been an important part of my life and I will always remember that, with pleasure. It is good that you are with your family, and I promise myself a great life ahead of me.'

---

[1] No, no, if you please Gérard. It's not necessary. You have your reasons, I know. I understand.

He took hold of both her hands and kissed each one in turn. 'Ah,' he told himself, 'she still uses Chanel 5.' And with that he was pleased.

They parted with mild regrets on both sides. To Gérard, it was the missed opportunity of a future liaison, which would put them on slightly different footings no doubt, but which promised to be exciting. The very features which appalled him when he first saw her from the market stalls have caused such a friction against his expectation that they had created sharp sparks of attraction in him. If there had not been a past, he might have made his move.

To Jacqueline, however, the future now would be of her own making. The onus of its success or failure would lie solely on her, and she was ready for the challenge. It was with the past that she had regrets. She had judged that Gérard had not loved her with the loyalty and devotion that was worth jeopardising her future for. The future remained a vague hypothesis of possibilities. But the past was a statement – a statement that she had failed as a woman, that so many years of her youth had been wasted. She could only brace herself and move forward, equipped with a better knowledge of men and of the world. But weighed against this was the frustration that it was impossible to go back and change the past.

> Le soleil, pourquoi brille-t-il
> À Caen,
> Ce jour, où l'impossibilité

Brûle mon cœur.[1]

'I can't remember when I last had such a delightful and satisfying day,' Jacqueline declared. 'Shall we do this again soon?' she added, smiling broadly at Michael. There was not the slightest coyness in her – just a spontaneous earnestness, which left Michael at ease.

'I'm always available on weekends. David goes back home each Friday afternoon. Just say when,' Michael replied.

'How about next Saturday?'

'Sure, what would you like to do?'

'You know what I fancy?' Jacqueline asked. 'Let's take the train into London and go to the theatre. Don't let's plan anything. Just take pot luck and see a play or a musical'

'That sounds great to me. I have been to concerts in London with my parents but I've not been to the theatre for a long while.'

That's settled then,' Jacqueline smiled. 'I would ask you to come up to my room, but I am in need of a shower. Let's make it the next time round.'

She leant forward and gave Michael a kiss on each cheek.

'Goodnight, Michael.'

'Goodnight.'

---

[1] The sun, why does it shine at Caen, on this day, when impossibility burns at my heart.

Just two light touches on his cheeks and he felt a tingling all down his spine. As she walked away, he was conscious that he was blushing. It was just a peck on the cheek, so why this sensation? What was it about Jacqueline? She certainly was not the prettiest or the sexiest person he had encountered. She was an enigma. He could not place her. There was something knowing about her, which made him feel that she understood what he was about and, sometimes, that she understood more than he was aware of himself. At other times, she was childlike in her responses.

He liked her laugh, always fulsome and to the point. That she did not giggle was a plus for Michael. Giggles, especially the high pitched, rippling kind, set him on edge. He considered them vacuous and a sign of attention seeking of an inferior, unsophisticated nature. He could see their raison d'être though – that so many men were susceptible to them.

They took the train from Watford Junction to Euston. From Gower Street they made their way briskly to Covent Garden where they stopped for a coffee, listening and watching two young violinists with Vivaldi on their strings. A slow stroll through St James's Park took them to Buckingham Palace. Crossing Westminster Bridge they arrived at the South Bank and Michael promised he would take Jacqueline to a concert at the Festival Hall one weekend. Hurrying over Hungerford Bridge against a gusty, icy wind they then traversed Trafalgar Square and soon arrived at the

West End. They managed to buy discount tickets for the matinee show of *Jesus Christ Superstar*.

Dinner was in China Town before they took the train back to Watford. Michael was adept at using the chopsticks, but Jacqueline was hesitantly game at trying them. It was an enjoyable, light-weight day of little moments, but they had bonded. When they parted that night Jacqueline was satisfied with a day un-wasted, but within Michael there welled youthful promises of further shared diversions.

They met up most Saturdays or Sundays and on each occasion discovered something new and interesting about each other. There was so much in common in their taste, humour and energy that any subtle differences and her vastly greater experience of life had set off a heightened moiré of interaction.

They invited Clinger out with them sometimes. It was a relief to Michael that Jacqueline and Clinger got on so well. There was an occasional tinge of guilt that he had not been around her as much as before, although he knew that she was seldom without the company of College friends.

Michael dropped in often at Jacqueline's room during the day and she might walk back with him to his house at weekends. Sometimes Jacqueline would read to him under a beech tree in the park or sitting in the armchair in her room while he lay on her bed. They would discuss college work or listen to music and Michael might strum on his guitar if they were at number 26. Except for when he walked back with them from College to the YMCA, David was out of the picture in this relationship. He was always amusing and comradely when Jacqueline was around, but it had never occurred to him to think of her as anything but a college-mate. She was not the young, pretty girl that would interest him. His world belonged to Gloria at weekends and to his friends during the week. Nobody could have been more content than he.

One evening in early November, Michael called by Jacqueline's room unusually around 8pm to return a book. In the past months, he had only ever been to her room in the daytime, sometimes leaving just before 6pm so that she could get ready to go downstairs to have dinner at the dining hall.

He stood in the corridor by the open bedroom door watching silently the small gathering of Jacqueline's friends and acquaintances. Her room appeared to be an open house, with people coming, staying for a while and then leaving, while others were comfortably ensconced in a chair or on the bed or merely standing around, enjoying a can of beer or a cup of coffee. There was no central track to the conversations. Everybody seemed to be talking in different groups. Lars was in a corner strumming his guitar. Lyndsey, a YMCA girl he had met a couple of times was laughing with a Nigerian student. Jacqueline was sitting on the bed with a man's arm around her waist. The air was smoky and heavy and if the window had not been left open, Michael might have found it unbearable. Everyone seemed to be relaxed. Michael felt he had intruded into an alien space.

'Are you OK?' Jacqueline whispered to Michael. 'You know some of the people here.'

'I'm fine. I'm quite happy people watching,' he replied, unwilling to make his excuses and leave. 'I'll join Lars in a moment.'

He was afraid Jacqueline might find him boring and a spoil sport. What was different between that night and any other situation he had encountered? Established the facts, got an idea of who was present, approached a couple of them and made a couple of comments, then watched them carry on from there. He might interject every now and again, preferably in agreement. He could always moot a point of mild contention and then leave the others to debate it. People were not really interested in what others had to say, as long as they were given the opportunity to hear themselves. Play it cool, Michael, play it cool.

He went over and sat on the floor, next to Lars. They chatted a little about guitars and agreed to play a round of squash the following week. Lars talked a little about how he missed the skiing in Norway. Chris Green came over and, being now in a group of his own, Michael relaxed a little and found the evening agreeable, but it was still an evening a distance from Jacqueline.

Soon after 9pm, people started to leave. Jacqueline was asked if she would like to go to the pub but she politely declined. Michael found himself stranded, listening to Lars and Chris discussing a chord on the guitar.

'Khas, do you know Lars, Chris and Michael?' Jacqueline asked.

'Only Chris,' he replied and shook everyone's hand as Michael looked up at the new arrival.

Very tall, very good looking and with long, wavy hair, Khas was the epitome Byronic[1] character. With his Irish Middle Eastern features and his soft spoken manner, he conjured up the image of a poetic lover, of an exotic species concocted by nature for one purpose – that of pleasing women. Michael had to look down as Jacqueline stood there with Khas' arm around her. An unexpected, portentous fear alarmed him.

Chris and Lars left, as though they knew it was time. Michael found himself sitting cross-legged on the floor with Jacqueline and Khas towering over him. He was in an indefensible position. He was the runt when he had wanted to be the leader of the pack. As if she understood his situation and wanting to relieve him of it, Jacqueline stretched out her hand to Michael. He took it and stood up, feeling a fool, being aided in front of Khas. Jacqueline kissed him goodnight on his cheek and whispered, 'I'll see you on Saturday.' Here indeed was a Queen dismissing majestically her courtier. He shook Khas' hand and said goodnight, withdrawing from the room where there was nowhere else he would rather be.

---

[1] Reference to Lord Byron, the Romantic Poet

He had had brief sexual experiences towards the end of his school days at St Alban. The first was with Sharon Wates, a girl from a neighbouring school. Everybody else had her, so he tried his luck. That encounter, however, he discounted. It was not a challenge and it had no value content. He did feel sorry for her. A very attractive girl, who thought she was popular because every boy could avail himself of her. But she will learn, she will grow up, he thought. We all grow up don't we? We all learn don't we?

The longest relationship he had lasted 3 months. Lorraine Pendleton was a charming and pretty girl. She was intelligent and sensible and to Michael the sort of girl one would marry. However, Lorraine was University bound and they had agreed that they were too young to have their freedom curtailed by each other. Besides, Lorraine was a Doctor's daughter and he had no relish to be embroiled again with the kind of family background he had been trying to escape.

There was something sensual and assured in the way Khas had held Jacqueline around the waist. Michael knew that Jacqueline had a colourful past. That knowledge had enthralled him and he had held it almost as a mystifying possession from which he could draw mentally, but from a distance in time and space, the occasional vignette of her life.

Their time together had been so warm, so delightful, so of one mind. Now he had seen other possibilities, and those were evolving without him. For that night, Khas would be the possessor and Michael the cast-off, to slouch away like a dog that had been kicked in the bollocks.

Jacqueline had had many lovers. Perhaps this was as insignificant as the others.

He did not notice the clear sky or the sparkling early frost on the road, or where he was going. The rumbling roll of the train above him shook him back to reality. He found himself walking under the railway bridge just outside Bushey[1]. Everything was depressing. What was he doing at Bushey? He was restless. He would seek out David. He would go to the *Coach Maker*. What did he care if Jacqueline and Khas fucked the night away? But he would care so much, so much if, after their love-making, they lay there in bed, talking, sharing thoughts. That embittered him.

'Michael!' Clinger exclaimed. It was unusual to see him at the *Coach Maker* at mid-week.

'Hiya,' he responded, looking around for David.

'David's gone to the kebab shop,' Clinger volunteered.

'I can't stay here, Clinger. How about I buy you a Chinese meal at *Four Seasons*?'

He got hold of her hand and led her out. Clinger did not question his action. She felt Michael was upset about something and was happy to be there for him. They walked along in silence with Clinger, clinging on

---

[1] Small town abutting Watford

to Michael's arm, trying to keep pace with his long strides.

'So sorry, Clinger,' Michael laughed when he noticed how fast he was going and how comically she was holding on to him. 'We are a right pair aren't we?'

'Come here,' he said, slowing down and putting his arm around her.

The Four Seasons was almost empty by the time they got there. The mid-week casual customers had come and gone. Michael asked for a table right in the corner at the back of the restaurant, which did not surprise Clinger. He pulled the chair out for her and saw that she was seated comfortably before going round to his seat. What always impressed Clinger were his good manners, which were unobtrusive and bred in him rather than recently learned and put into practice to impress.

In spite of all the qualities which David had loved in him – his good look, his apparent ease with people, his quiet self-control and his intelligence – what Clinger discerned was his vulnerability. This touched her enormously as if she, who considered herself dumpy and plain, had had an access into the soul of this gorgeous man whom she adored. She had always perceived him as an outsider looking in whenever they were in a crowd or among friends. She wanted to fold him into her arms and say, 'There, there, it's alright. It's not so bad.'

Michael suggested they ordered the food the Chinese way. He suggested having plain rice, the beef with green peppers and black bean sauce, the sweet and sour pork, which he knew Clinger loved, and the 3 seafood fried noodles – all to share between them. There was a pot of Chinese tea for him and a glass of red for her.

'So what's up?' she asked.

'Nothing and everything,' Michael replied as he adeptly picked up a slippery piece of beef. 'Let's enjoy the food for now,' he added, smiling at her.

The Parade, at one end of the High Street, was quite deserted by 11 pm except for a few stragglers leaving the pubs. It had turned surprisingly cold and a fine layer of sparkling frost had formed on the concrete ledges of the raised rectangular pond which ran along the middle of the Parade, dividing it into two sides. A few ducks swam away across the pond as Michael and Clinger sat on a ledge.

'What's wrong, Michael,' Clinger asked.

Michael did not respond. Clinger was not certain whether he had heard her, but did not repeat the question. Michael got up, turned around and faced her. Opening up his feeling and his thoughts was obviously very difficult for him. He normally held his own counsel. He certainly would not have thought it prudent to speak out to David or to anyone else, but he liked Clinger, always felt comfortable with her and trusted her.

'I'm scared, Clinger. I don't know why, but I'm scared. I've always thought life should be lived as an adventure – one takes what comes and makes of it what one can. If one has no fixed goal, then one could not go too far astray,' he declared, looking fixedly at Clinger, but at a point sharply beyond her.

'What's happened?' she enquired

'Nothing eventful. It's laughable. I can only tell this to you, Clinger. You won't laugh or think me peculiar. This evening, I went up to Jacqueline's room and everything was fine. There were lots of people coming and going. Everybody seemed quite at home there. I'd never expected this. I always left her room before dinner time. You know, it added another dimension to her. Then, when most people had left, this bloke, Khas, arrived. You can tell when there is something going on between people. I felt that between them. I wanted to stay and see how it turned out, but somehow I felt redundant, in the way. Lars and Chris Green were there with me and they left almost as a matter of course. Why did I feel so humiliated, so down-trodden, when I knew I had to leave? It was as if she had dismissed me.'

Michael sat down again and took Clingers hand.

'You are cold. How thoughtless of me,' he apologised.

'I'm alright. I have many layers on me,' Clinger said, not wishing this rare intimacy from Michael to stop.

'I'm just twenty and the last thing I need is to be emotionally tied to anyone. We've had some lovely time together, Jacqueline and I, but I'd never thought beyond that. All at once I'm scared of losing her. But, you know, I'm even more scared of feeling this way.

Life's pattern shouldn't be set when one is twenty. Perhaps somewhere in the future there would be that right woman for me. I don't think Jacqueline is the one, but she is the one I want right now and I feel I cannot do without her. Is that frightening or what?' he exclaimed and then laughed.

'What about you, Clinger, have you ever had such crazy feelings for anyone?'

'Of course, but when you are not pretty, you soon learn not to have too many flights of fancy. But I'm not despondent. Like you, I know that somewhere there is someone for me. I'm not talking of someone ideologically ideal, but someone who will happen along. There must be. I need to be a mother,' she said jokingly.

'And I'm certain you will be. You know, I always thought of you as someone very attractive and warm and kind.'

'Ah! but not as someone to fall madly in love with. But why are you so troubled by Jacqueline? You are a great looking guy and you are a steady friend. People like you normally go through life from one good experience to another.'

'I'm not so sure about being good-looking. I've never really been popular like David. He gets on so well with everybody. I find him quite delightful. There is something missing in me.' Michael appeared genuinely perplexed that Clinger had found him good looking. Nobody had ever said that to him before. Clinger was laughing.

'What?' Michael asked.

'The way you said – David is quite delightful. People don't say things like that these days. You say someone is a great guy, or that he is a joker or something non-committal like that. But that's what I like about you. Oh, David is the joker in the pack. He is so funny. But sometimes a girl likes a little of the serious in a man. I'll put my cards on the table with you, Michael. I'd fancied you ever since we first met,' she chuckled, making light of what she had said.

'Have you? Thank you,' he answered awkwardly. I'm so lucky to have you as my friend,' he smiled. Bending slightly towards her, he put his arms around her and kissed her lingeringly on the lips. In the frosty night, he enjoyed the warmth of her in his arms. What she felt, he was completely unaware of. He put a hand on her elbow and helped her up and held her close around the waist as he walked her home. That Clinger could have felt so much affection for him touched him deeply. But his heart was elsewhere, troubled by Jacqueline.

The house was cold on his return and there was a freshness to his pillows which should induce sleep, but sleep would not come. He worried that David, who had not come back, was spending too much time away from his studies. The uncertainties regarding Jacqueline were so deep-rooted by then that he was not even conscious of their presence. He felt calm, but a little embarrassed by the earlier exhibition of his feelings. He switched on his bedside light and picked up a book of short stories Jacqueline had lent to him. He turned to Andre Gide's *Le Retour de l'Enfant Prodigue*[1] and read on from where he had left off. Like the Prodigal Son returned, he felt a despondent weakling, and he had not even started on his journey yet.

The shutting of the front door woke him. He followed David's soft footsteps up the stairs and into his bed-room. He could hear movement there. David now on his bed.

Even towards the end of November scarcely any rain had fallen. What managed to relieve a little the long, dry summer was a fine, gentle drizzle which hardly remained on what it touched before evaporating. The ground stayed dry and hard. The last Friday of the month, however, brought with it a heavier fall with a stronger accompanying breeze which felt bitter after the prolonged Indian summer which had preceded it. In this uncomfortable weather Jacqueline was walking away from college, sheltered by a small umbrella, towards the shops. From behind her, a strong sturdy arm craned around her waist and she turned in stunned surprise to discover David walking alongside her.

'Oh! Hello!' She laughed. 'You are lucky I do not have a violent reflex.'

---

[1] The Return of the Prodigal Son

'Oh, it's you,' David teased, 'what are you doing sharing my umbrella! Actually I was getting a little wet. You don't mind?'

'Since it's you, I promise not to mind.'

'Since it's me who is the little devil, let me buy you a drink. Let's get out of the rain,' he suggested, leading her towards *Kardomah*.[1] 'What would you have? Tea, coffee, a soft drink? No brandy here I'm afraid.'

'A brandy would be a fine thing after the shock you had given me, but a black coffee would do.'

'Would you like a slice of cake or something?'

'How about an Eccles cake?'

'Now, am I forgiven?' David asked after ordering the drinks and cakes.

'You'll have your come-uppance one of these days. I might have swung out and hit you right on the nose.'

'I know you wouldn't, you're too sweet,' said David with that broad, boyish, innocent grin of his.

'I thought you would be on your way home by now. Michael said you go back every Friday.'

'Used to, but not every Friday now. I have a birthday party to go to tonight.'

'To Natalie's?' she asked.

'That's right. I see you've been invited too.'

'Yes. In fact I can't stay too long here. I was on my way to get her a gift before *Clements*[2] closes. What are you getting her?'

---

[1] A tea-room/cafe
[2] A departmental Store

'A couple of six packs.'

'You can't give a girl six packs of lager on her birthday, for goodness sake,' Jacqueline laughed.

'Oh, I don't know, girls are tough these days,' he retorted. 'Rough and ready, you know,' he beamed.

'Well, I must be going. Would you like to walk part of the way with me? Nothing to stop you getting wet after that though.'

'Tell you what, I'll walk with you and as a thank you, you could let me take you to Natalie's tonight.'

'Michael would be coming for me, but you could come along.'

'Oh, that'll make a fine crowd,' he laughed.

It occurred to Jacqueline that that was the sort of comment which Michael might have made. She smiled at him and thought it might be fun having him with her for a little longer.

Michael had expected David to join him and Jacqueline all along. Not one to throw himself into the exuberance of a youthful party, he found the ease with which David could assimilate himself in a crowd quite comforting. Somehow, he too, being generally associated with David, had vicariously become a part of the event.

The overcast sky could not dampen David's spirit. The rain had long stopped, but the persistent cover of cloud prevented the cold air from chilling into frost. They got to the party after nine, having stopped at a pub on the way. They were joined by Sandra Cooke, a girl from Jacqueline's class, and her boyfriend, Geoff

Trewin from the College of Art. Together with Jorge and his girlfriend, they marched along, arms linked, high kicking and singing to '*You Made Me Love You, I didn't Want To Do It*', much to Michael's amusement. He walked behind a little sheepishly, embarrassed by what passers-by might think, but finding the spectacle strangely quaint – like a postcard of yesteryears of people enjoying themselves in more innocent times.

Jacqueline excused herself and waited for Michael to catch up.

'Come on,' she said coaxingly, 'loosen up a little.' She held him by the arm and led him along in an understated skip, knowing how uncomfortable he must be, but wishing him to be a part of the party. She remembered the confident charm of Gérard which had won her over with its enthusiasm and eagerness to impress. She remembered how shy she had been when confronted by Gérard. But Michael was outwardly confident, though in a more mature and quieter way – so why the reticence and the inability to join in the fun? She found that puzzling.

Although always civil and attentive to others, the real Michael was rather unapproachable. Perhaps what made David's relationship with him so successful was that David had no inclination to try to understand him at all. He was just his friend, just Michael. All this delving and digging into the psychology of a situation was completely unnecessary in his world.

The party was in full swing. Almost everyone in Natalie's inner and outer circle of friends seemed to be there. The house was packed, the music blared and the drinks flowed freely. Cigarette smoke softly veiled these happy, happy spectral people. Yet there he stood, Michael, almost hastening time away.

In a corner by a table lamp, Clinger was at the cassette player selecting a cassette. Michael joined her but did not interfere with her choice. They sat together on the floor sharing a joint. Jacqueline and David were with Natalie and a few other girls, looking at her presents. A couple was in the middle of the room attempting, sort of a dance. Somebody came over and switched off the table light and from the kitchen somebody else carried through a birthday cake with its candles lit and the girls screamed with delight as if that was the last thing they had expected to see. Clinger clutched at Michael and told him that she was feeling rough. She had not felt very well the whole evening. Probably the kebab she ate before coming. Michael went upstairs with her where she was sick.

The cake had been cut by the time they came downstairs. Some couples were dancing. Michael interrupted David and Jacqueline and explained that he was taking Clinger home. He told David to Make sure Jacqueline was alright and to take her back to the YMCA. He insisted on ringing up for a cab even though Clinger, who appeared ashen and unsteady, said she would be OK. He felt guilty that he had not realised she was unwell when he shared the joint with her. It must have aggravated her condition.

He had not missed being at the party, but felt he had let Jacqueline down. He had not been good company. In fact he had not been company at all to her. Before Clinger could reach her bedroom, she was retching and just got to the bathroom in time to be sick again. Michael settled her in bed, brought some hot water from the kitchen and gave her 2 Paracetamols. When she had fallen asleep, he shut his eyes and was asleep soon in the chair by her bedside.

It was past 2 in the morning before Clinger's house-mates returned from the party. Michael stayed for a coffee. He refused their offer of the sofa and decided to walk back. The sky had cleared and faintly displayed a few twinkling stars. On the road, fine, sharp, crystalline frost under the streetlights out-sparkled the stars. He felt alone.

The house was in the dark when he entered it. He did not switch on the light in case it might wake David. At the top of the stairs he noticed that David's door was still open. He knew then that he had not returned. He turned back downstairs and switched the hall light on for David before going back up to his room. He threw himself onto his bed, and he tried, so hard to sleep.

That night David did not come back. Ah, Michael thought, life would have its twist.

His mind was untrained to compartmentalise and then to leave each compartment aside, shelved, to gather dust, never to germinate. His mind was trained to compartmentalise, to analyse, to find links, to create a flow of understanding, to create a meadow from where he could glean. But if the harvest promised to be bitter, which way should he turn? With the first morning glow from his window, he woke with just one question – 'WHY?' resounding in his mind. It was just there like an instinctive animal warning. He was trapped. Which way was he to turn? Why was turning imperative? Had a decision to be made?

After a shower, he went downstairs and had a coffee. Then, back in his room, he sat down at his study table and wrote a short note for David. He put on warm clothes and his leather jacket and, kick-starting his Yamaha, he rode away towards home.

It was not that he was drawn towards home, the idea quite repulsed him, but there was just nowhere else he felt he could go. He was ashamed that he had loved. He was ashamed that his heart could be broken. And home, isn't it a nest? Isn't it where children run back to until they have grown, until they have matured and become sensible adults? He deserved nowhere better.

After enjoying an unusually long, hot summer, succeeded by an almost seamless Indian summer, many people, that end of 1976, in a knowingly British way, were predicting a bitter winter. But that year winter did not come with a ferocious vengeance. Towards the middle of December it had turned gradually colder without excessive frost or any gathering of gales or beating downpours.

On the morning of Friday, 17th December, however, Watford woke up to a thin covering of fine snow that had fallen silently through the still night, to take enchantingly the town by surprise. It was a week day and children were on their way to school, shop assistants hurried as best they could to the centre of town and the traffic snarled. David made his first snowball and aimed it at Michael, who dodged and threw one back at him. And they smiled, as only youths could smile, carefree in the falling snow. They were disappointed that Jacqueline had already left for college. David was all for taking the day off, but was persuaded to continue on his way to college.

'I am playing squash after class and Jacqueline is going out with some YM people to see *Mrs Warren's Profession*[1] at The Palace,' Michael explained why they could not go to the park after class.

'If the snow sticks we could get up early tomorrow and get there before the kids – what do you say?'

'You think it will stick?' David asked.

'It certainly is cold enough. We'll ask Jacqueline to come with us.'

'She didn't mention going to the play to me last night,' David said.

'Nor to me. She doesn't have to tell us everything, you know, you silly boy.'

It was still dark when David got up and shook Michael awake. The snow had settled and he was eager

---

[1] A play by George Bernard Shaw

to get going. Michael insisted on having his coffee and cereal first. They sat in the dining room and breakfasted.

'Jacqueline might not be up. How are you going to let her know you are there?'

'Oh, I'll ask someone in the kitchen to go up and call her,' David replied smugly. 'I know my way around.'

Cassiobury Park was almost pristine from overnight snowfall when they got there. There were a few tracks made probably by cats or, further along, by a lone fox. Along the long straight path that started from the edge of the road itself, there were signs of a few people having gone that way. The tall trunks of the beech tress stretched upwards in smooth, grey melancholy before unfolding their branches rather untidily upwards. The old oaks, gnarled to their roots, took on a sturdier, heraldic stance. Further on, a few conifers, perhaps a fir or a yew, dusted with snow, appeared sombre, their leaves looking almost charcoal in the early light against the whiteness of the snow.

'This is what I love so much about the snow here. It comes so rarely, but when it does, it creates such charming scenes. On the mountains there is a uniformity of snow and pine trees. They may be awe-inspiring but they lack the charm we see here.' Jacqueline exclaimed. 'We know it is not going to last, so we want to rush out and play in it.'

'There is something sad about snow, so soft and fragile, unable to survive very long,' Michael added.

'Don't get bloody serious. I love the snow,' David shouted as he made a snowball and threw it at Michael, who made an even larger one and, together with Jacqueline, chased David, threw it at his back, and then tackled him down, rubbing handfuls of snow on his head. In retaliation, David rolled him over and calling for Jacqueline's help, pinned him down and, with a free hand, covered his face with snow.

Jacqueline noticed how dark and long Michael's lashes were, accentuated by the flakes of snow on them. Lying there, with his eyes shut and a smile on his face, he looked beatified, a saint, in an eternal rest upon a pure sea of white. And then she turned a little and there was David, much fairer, a robust presence, his cheeks ruddy from the play along the way, an earthling without question. And they laughed and they lay on the snow.

David wanted to build a snowman and began scooping the snow right down to the grass with both his hands. He was immediately reprimanded by Jacqueline, who showed him how to compress the snow into a small ball and then to roll it along, gathering the top layer of snow as it went along. It all sounded like too much hard work, so David hastily piled one small ball on top of another and, with bits broken off from a fallen beech twig, he stuck in the eyes and nose and finished off the job with a curved gash with his index finger.

For a brief moment, Michael wondered what Clinger was doing then. If it had been the year before, he would have gone and brought her to the park and they would probably have made a snowman too. He felt a little guilty but at the same time he felt so carefree and relaxed. He brushed away the snow from his clothes and suggested they walked on to the Grand Union Canal since the park had by then become a playground full of screaming children, full of parents and dogs. Jacqueline agreed without hesitation.

Michael was right, Jacqueline thought – there was something sad about snow. That day at Düsseldorf had started clear but icy sharp with the wind that blew across the Rhine. Then the wind ceased and large, soft flakes of snow descended like curtains upon the past, curtains which obliterated what was without revealing what would be. She felt justified in her recrimination. She was on her own. She had lost both Edward and her mother. Somewhere in the world was her father, perhaps at home, perhaps in London, perhaps in America. She had not forgiven him. From that night when he hit her so hard she miscarried Gérard's baby, she had written him out of her life. Her mother had occasionally mentioned him, but she had taken no interest in whatever she had said. And now when she had needed a friend, a friend to hold out a hand to lift her, a friend to hear her cry, a friend to point the way, Gérard had failed her.

She pulled her coat closer to her. She was going to walk through all that snow and come out the other side. She would find a way.

Yes, Michael was probably right, there was something sad about the snow.

Through the dimples in the glass window at *Kardomah*, Clinger saw them approaching – the three of them. Michael had his arm around Jacqueline, while David, gesticulating, appeared to be cracking some joke which sent the other two doubling up in laughter. They were never going to be lovers, Michael and she. She had no illusion of that, but they had been close and she missed that special friendship they had shared. If only she could understand what was going on. It used to be just Michael and Jacqueline but, of late, David appeared more and more part of the scene. She knew Michael was besotted with her, but the murmurs seemed to link her with David. It was not her place to sound Michael about this, but she was afraid for him. She could not bear him to be hurt. How tender, how sensitive he was.

She turned back to Natalie and Jayne, hoping that she had not betrayed her emotion. She heard them when they entered *Kardomah* and was glad she was facing away from them, but Michael came over to say hello to them.

Fortunately, they had finished their drinks and Clinger suggested they should get on with their shopping.

'Well, I'll see you next week then,' Michael said to Clinger.

'I shan't be here next week,' Clinger replied, 'I am taking a few days' French leave. My mother will be in London and I'll be meeting her there before going to Amsterdam with her to see my brother and his new baby. So I'll see you in the new year. What about you? What would you be doing over Christmas?'

'Like you, I will be with my parents. They have been invited by friends in Germany to attend a few concerts at Bayreuth. I might get back before they do. David's invited me over for New Year Eve. Have a great Christmas then,' he said, giving her a hug. 'I'll come and see you when we get back.'

Of the three girls there, Michael would have chosen to be with Clinger anytime. He felt that Clinger was wrong to have so little confidence in herself. It was true that Natalie was very pretty, in a big, blue eyed, curly hair, lustrous skin and bubbly manner. But she was apparently aware of it and used it in an inoffensive flirty way and was very popular.

Jayne was a picture of health, with her hair pulled back, her figure well-proportioned and strong, and her warm but slightly reserved smile. She was excellent at sports and had beaten Michael in squash often enough. From a background not dissimilar to Michael's, she was well-spoken and always reminded Michael of a head prefect in a girl's school. If anything needed managing, Jayne would be the one to seek out. Michael could imagine her running a family of well-brought-up straight-laced children and running a husband in a high earning job or position.

But it would be with Clinger that Michael would rather spend time. She had the ingenuous disposition of someone who believed that she had neither the tool of beauty nor of great intellect to be artful with. Everybody called her Clinger and she laughed and accepted it. There was no vanity to be diminished by it. One felt comfortable in her company. Michael could not imagine Jacqueline tolerating such an appellation. But then he could not imagine anyone regarding Jacqueline in that way. They might be censorious of her, or dislike her, or admire her, but they certainly would not take her lightly.

That evening Michael prepared steaks. They had been to the shops and the market and had come back with *The Times* and *Daily Express*. While David looked through the papers, Jacqueline helped to prepare the vegetables before Michael could persuade her to leave the cold kitchen to join David. It would be a simple meal before they went off to the *Coach Maker*. Being the last Saturday before the Christmas break, they were bound to meet up with other college friends. On this occasion, Michael was all for it. He thought he might see Clinger there and have a few quiet words with her.

The steaks were to be simply grilled and served with some French beans, carrots and boiled potatoes. He seasoned the meat juices and stirred in some crushed pepper and cream for the sauce. After a long day out, he knew David would be famished.

From his room he brought down a bottle of red wine for Jacqueline and him and gave David a can of lager. Jacqueline was pleased but not surprised at Michael's ability to cook, the steak being just about rare. Gérard was a good cook and many of the men she knew in Germany and France were quite capable of coming up with quick, tasty dishes. To David, who never had to prepare food at home, Michael was a wonder. He was constantly astonished at what Michael came up with. In his own life there had never been any occasion or need to learn how to cook.

Dinner over, David and Jacqueline volunteered to wash up. Then they freshened up and slushed their way to the *Coach Maker* through thawing snow. Through the window of the pub they could see that there was a large crowd that night, probably consisting of college students and folks from the YMCA. The whole atmosphere was convivial. In a quieter way, Jacqueline fitted in readily and was soon chatting lightly with several men.

Michael could not find Clinger and was disappointed. He expected her to be there on the last Saturday before term ended. A touch of guilt and shame passed through him. He felt she was avoiding him, or rather avoiding the situation of being with him and Jacqueline in the pub. He felt inclined to go and call on her but couldn't bear to leave Jacqueline and David. Soon he was approached by Lars and his mates and began to feel more comfortable. Looking askance at Jacqueline throughout the evening, he realised that he was never going to have her to himself in a crowd of friends.

They stopped by at the YMCA for Jacqueline to pack an overnight bag on their way back. It was close to midnight when they got in to the cold house. Michael hastened to switch on the electric fire in the sitting room and in the dining room. Upstairs, he switched on the wall fire above the mirror in the bathroom and brought out a fresh towel and a small tablet of hotel soap for Jacqueline, offering his own room for her use. David had slumped heavily onto the sofa and was soon asleep.

While Jacqueline washed herself upstairs, Michael prepared some sandwiches and left them in the dining room. He put a cassette in the player and then sat on the bean bag and waited for Jacqueline.

The electric fire threw a still, warm glow on the room but Michael felt uneasy. He was on the high sea, on a boat travelling away from his childhood and from innocence. There were other players on the boat with whom he had cohered, from whom he had drawn sustenance. When the boat arrived, where would these people be? Would their lives continue to be attached or would they be flung apart? When the summer ended the following year, what would life present to him? Did he have the resource and the worldliness to shape his future, or would his future fall the way a die falls, on the whim of chance?

He went into the dining room and opened a bottle of red wine when he heard Jacqueline coming down the stairs. She had changed into a knee length black skirt and a black knitted top which was loose in spite of its fitted cut. Her hair had been brushed and glowed in the light. They decided it was not necessary to disturb David and sat down to the sandwich and wine.

It had been some time since Michael had been alone with Jacqueline. That she had just come out of the shower, her hair freshly brushed, dressed for indoors, sitting quietly with him having a sandwich, lent an air of intimacy to the scene. He felt close to her again.

'My parents have asked me to go with them to Bayreuth for Christmas. They have been invited to some Wagner concerts there. Would you be going away?'

'No, not this time. I have lots to sort out at home. The house needs a good clean and there are lots of stuff to clear out.'

'You'll be on your own?' Michael asked.

'Yes, but I don't mind. I don't make a fuss about Christmas or the New Year. When Gérard was around we used to invite Edward, who lived next door, to come over for a meal on Christmas day. We might have a joint of beef or pork or even fish. Gérard couldn't stand turkey. After he had left, I continued to have Edward over until he died.'

'What was he like, Edward?'

'A very gentle, very well-read and cynical man. He was in his late sixties when we first knew him. He was a retired lecturer in English from somewhere in East Anglia. He left his wife and sons to follow a woman to Reading but she passed away quite soon after. I'd learned so much from him. Many an evening we would sit either at his place or mine and he would tell me so much about books and poetry. My knowledge of literature really stopped in the fifties, perhaps a little into the sixties.'

'You must miss him,' Michael suggested.

'Not as much as you might think. You see, he had already given me all that he could give and that remains with me. So in a way he is always a part of me, much more so than Gérard is.'

How marvellous he looks, she thought as she looked at Michael. Not just in his features but in the sincere eagerness he showed in his eyes as he questioned her. There was something unsettled, something anxious, something desirous of answers in them that interested her. She detected a great depth in him which was still a depth of void, by the law of nature waiting and demanding to be filled. She wanted to reach out to him, to that indefinable sadness that he had found in the fall of snow. There was little that he had to say of himself. But then he was young, so young, and it was better that he had not prattled on about insignificant nothingness than to have puffed with confidence about himself.

While Michael cleared the table, Jacqueline returned to the sitting room. David was still sprawled out on the sofa fast asleep. She put down her glass of wine on the coffee table and looked through the collection of cassettes on the floor by the fire and picked up *Chapter Two – Roberta Flack*. As she was getting up, Michael came in and, momentarily proffering an arm and then withdrawing it, he asked if she would dance with him.

'Of course,' Jacqueline smiled, surprised at being asked to dance by Michael, who had insisted before that he did not dance.

In fact he danced a slow dance very well indeed. 'No fling and flung for me' he said and laughed. It reminded Jacqueline of herself when Gérard first asked her to dance, oh so many years ago. This was the first time they had been physically close to each other. He gradually held her closer to him and they danced, hardly moving, through *The First Time Ever I Saw Your Face* and *Will You Still Love Me Tomorrow*.

'Jacqueline,' he whispered.

'Hmm?'

'Will you seduce me?' he asked softly, but not bashfully.

She moved away slightly and looked into his eyes. They were not pleading eyes. They were sincere. There was a barrier they had to break through in order for their relationship to progress. It puzzled her that Michael had even to ask. Most men would simply have started on it and allowed it to carry on willy-nilly. Some, less experienced and fresher to the game, might timidly ask if he could go all the way. Others, old hats, would have complacently arrived at the end of a routine and reached out for a cigarette before you have your second tingle.

It was as if Michael had ceded the power to her – you have the mastery, you have the experience, show me how. I shall enjoy it, but you play it your way. She smiled and, running a hand through his hair, she moved his head down a little and kissed him.

The faintest trace of perfume wafted by him and was gone just as quickly. He could not recall its fragrance yet he knew it well. It was like a vivid dream which, upon waking, could not be remembered. There was not even a loose thread to retrace it to its original fabric. He re-focussed on her. He felt the slimness of her body and the firm narrow waist. He was pleased that he had had sexual experiences before and that this was more than just that. He moved his hands under her knitted top to her curved back and un-fastened her bra. The bra had been in existence long enough for the male of the species to know instinctively how to undo it. Her breasts were firm and warm but he relaxed his hold in order to pull her tight against him. 'This is me, this is my hardness, this hardness desires you,' he seemed to proclaim.

David rolled over to one side. The world was a haze and, through half open eyes, he saw Jacqueline and Michael dancing. He sighed. Sitting up, he steadied himself before rising and drifting towards his friends.

'I want to dance,' he said and put his arms around them as they extended an arm each to embrace him.

'This is the happiest day of my life,' he said, as they shifted gently from side to side.

Leaning towards Michael, he kissed him on the lips. 'I love you Michael,' he murmured. Then turning to Jacqueline he kissed her. 'And I love you, Jacqueline,' he repeated. 'I've never been so happy. We're so complete. I can only think of in a nutshell, why? I don't know,' he added.

'I wan'te pee,' he said suddenly and, dropping his arms, he moved groggily away.

The incongruity to the whole situation and atmosphere made Michael and Jacqueline snigger and then they burst into laughter. Michael followed him out to switch on the stair light. When he got back, the magical bubble of romance mixed with testosterone had burst. Jacqueline was sitting on one of the bean bags drinking her wine and laughing still. In a rather gauche manner, David had endeared himself to both of them. *Tonight, I celebrate my love* Roberta sang.

Michael had pulled the other bean bag towards Jacqueline and they continued to drink, in silence, listening to the music. David came back and plonked himself heavily next to Jacqueline, wrapping a leg over her and resting his head against her and then promptly fell asleep. Michael wondered if he had washed his hands. He got up to switch off the stair light and, on getting back, realised that he was on his own on the other bag. He sat quietly, deep in thoughts, as Jacqueline too dropped off to sleep. '*The night is like a lovely tune, beware my foolish heart,*' Roberta warned.

Michael turned off the cassette which had ended and retrieved the wine glass from Jacqueline's hand, leaving it on the coffee table. He stood for a while in the glow and low hum of the electric fire, looking down at Jacqueline and David.

Then he seemed to have made up his mind and, leaving the sitting room, went up to David's room. He picked up the duvet from David's bed, shook it, folded it onto his arm and went back downstairs. He carefully covered Jacqueline and David with it and, stepping backward, he turned to switch off the electric fire. He hesitated for a moment in the sudden darkness, wondering if he should lie down on the sofa, but decided against it.

He poured the remaining red wine from the bottle into his glass. Without turning on the light, he found his way to the stairs. On the fourth step he stopped, took a sip, listened, and then continued coldly up to his room.

There is a tide in the affairs of men, which taken at the flood[1] … he … he understood.

Loser!

In a feverish tremble, he got into bed and lay awake.

---

[1] Williams Shakespeare – Brutus' speech in Julius Caesar

3 Homecoming

The alarm went. He was ready for it, stretching a hand out to hit decidedly the buzz button. Susan had been up for at least half an hour, waking him as she got out of bed. Now that she had turned off the shower, he could hear the rain beating against the window. He covered his head with a pillow as she opened the bathroom door, casting a column of light onto the bed.

'You'd better get up now if you want to miss the traffic,' she coaxed. He didn't respond. He would hit the M25[1] rush hour traffic at some stage or other, a few more minutes in bed won't do much harm. If only Susan would leave him alone instead of getting up before him every time he had to leave early. He didn't require breakfast before he left the house. There were motorway services on the way. His time was pretty much his own till mid-day.

'Would you like some eggs and toast? Or cereals?'

'No! Just a cup of coffee,' he replied.

---

[1] 117 miles of Motorway encircling much of Greater London. Also known as the London Orbital Motorway

'Well, go and shower then. I haven't got all day. I have things to do before getting to school,' she continued.

'You get on and do what you want. I can take care of the coffee,' he grumbled.

'Would you like me to make some sandwiches for you?'

'No Susan, I can stop at the services if I need anything. Just leave it.'

'Well, I think you should be up by now.'

'Yeah!'

She looked at him through the dressing table mirror, all cuddled up like a child, and her face softened. Perhaps a few more minutes won't matter. She wondered, as she defined her lips with a darker shade of red, if he had done his packing, having refused her offer the previous night. She had ironed his shirts and trousers and made sure that he had sufficient pants and socks, and laid them all on the table in the laundry room. She must check.

By the time he came down to the kitchen, she was almost ready to leave.

'Drink up your coffee. I'll wash the cup before I go.'

'Why are you so early? You're not the ruddy gate-keeper,' he complained.

'I've to stop by at Gavin's with his laundry.'

'Why can't Kellie take care of that? She's the bloody girlfriend isn't she?'

'You know what these young girls are like. They can't do anything properly. Gavin likes my ironing,' she said with pride.

'He can at least come and pick it up himself,' he said. 'Well, I'm off.' He got up and gave her a peck on the cheek.

'When will you be back? Thursday or Friday?'

'I don't know. Probably Friday.'

'Get back in good time then. Don't get stuck in the traffic like you did last month,'

'I'll get back,' he said.

'Don't forget we are going to the Priest Hole for the quiz night with Carol and Frank,' she reminded him. 'You want to take the quiz book with you?'

'Nah,' he said, giving her a hug, 'bye!' He looked out at the rain and cursed.

Forwarding 2 files across to Josh's computer, Denise then tidied up her desk and looked at herself in the small compact mirror. She applied a raspberry coloured lipstick to her lips, passing it across twice and finishing off by dabbing a piece of tissue over it. She walked across to Josh's desk and handed the hard copies of the files to him.

'Here you are Josh. If you need to add or alter anything, do it on these and I will enter the changes later. I am not expecting any call regarding these, except perhaps from Modus Instruments – just confirm the interview dates. Are you sure you won't come with us?'

'Yes. It is better for one of us to stay back in the office.'

'Well, I'll be off when he gets here. Please cover for me if I am a bit late. And thanks,' she said, moving across the room to Naomi at reception.

'Naomi, could you give me a shout if you see Mr. Chapman approaching? I'll be at the store-room.'

'Oh, he's lovely isn't he?' Naomi smiled approvingly, to which Denise did not deign to respond. She held the distinction between Josh and herself, who had been with the company a long time and who could be familiar with each other, and those who were relatively new, especially someone like Naomi, who had only been there a few months.

The heavier rain of the early morning had eased into an intermittent fine drizzle and then stopped suddenly, leaving the sky a bluish grey, but hiding still the summer sun. David discarded his light polyester jacket on the back of his office chair and, deciding that it was unlikely that he would require his sun glasses, left them on his desk. He told Marisa, his new PA, that he would be out for a couple of hours and was not expecting any important calls. Then, running steadily down the stairs, he left the office at Horseshoe Park and walked towards Pangbourne[1].

He liked the feel of the small town and the people he had met had been friendly. Over the previous 3 months he had set up his small office and with the help

---

[1] A small town on the River Thames in West Berkshire

of *Accent Recruitment* had employed Marisa to oversee the office and to act as his personal assistant. Then they had found for him a graphic artist and a field representative to cover the M4[1] from South London to Bristol. As a thank you gesture he had invited Josh and Denise for lunch.

When he arrived, Naomi was away from the reception. He saw Josh and went over to him.

'Josh, ready to go?' he asked.

'Thank you David, but I am not able to do it today. The boss is out and only one of us can go with you, so I asked Denise to do the honour,' he explained.

'That's too bad, but we could get together some other time.'

'I've 3 interviews lined up for you for tomorrow. There's a chap called Grant from Farnham, who seems really suitable for what you need. The other 2 are from Basingstoke and Guildford. If you have the time after lunch, shall we go over their CVs?'

'Sure, let's do that,' he agreed.

He saw Denise coming from the back office and he liked what he saw. In his view, a woman who did not know how to put on her make-up, was a woman who did not bother about herself and why should a man bother about her? He liked the glossy redness of her lips and the wavy thickness of her mid blonde hair. Her eyes were subtly shadowed in blues and greys. He

---

[1] Motorway 4 West of London in the direction of Wales

guessed she must be in her late forties, but what a looker.

She was exasperated that nobody had called her. She hated to keep anyone waiting. She apologised profusely even though David explained that he had not been there long and that he had things to discuss with Josh. Women! He thought to himself and liked them even more for what they were.

He did not require women to be clever, for he did not consider himself to be clever. As long as they were pleasant to the eyes and not insipid, he could cope. Contrary to this notion, his wife Susan, considered beautiful by many, was an intelligent woman. She held a good degree and qualifications in teacher training. Unbeknown to him she had managed their relationship so deftly that, although he might be often irritated by her ways, he simply adored her. She was a physical woman, she knew her place, she was house-proud and a good mother. In over twenty years of their marriage, he had not once been unfaithful to her. This was not necessarily an achievement. Although extremely popular and attractive to women and loving their company, he had all he needed conveniently at home. He did not have to try to be faithful. No Herculean task existed for him to overcome. He was happily a basic man with basic needs.

He was disappointed that Josh could not leave the office. He thought it would be less complicated if he were with both of them. A short distance away around the corner of the road was the old roadside inn, *The*

Cross Keys. Hidden at the back was a covered area at the edge of the Pang, a small clear stream that, in a few hundred yards, would flow into the Thames. He had been there once before on his walk-about in the area before purchasing the lease on the office. He thought it was a charming and quiet corner for a little chat and an opportunity to get to know Denise and Josh a little better.

Denise had ordered an egg and cress sandwich and a diet coke, keeping to her resolution not to have anything too heavy at lunchtime. After looking at the menu, David decided to have a club sandwich as a fair balance to her sandwich. He ate out every evening that he was at Pangbourne and he could go for something more substantial then.

'You and Josh seem to run the show at *Accent Recruitment*,' David suggested.

'We are the most senior people. Josh has been with us about seven years and I have been there forever. Louise whom you must have met joined us 2 years ago from another agency. Yes, we are a good team. I can't see me going anywhere else now.'

'You must have a good boss for you and Josh to stay so long. People tend to move around a lot these days.'

'I must admit she has been very good to me. She's the type who'll leave you to get on with it once you've gained her trust.'

'Do you specialise in different areas of recruitment?'

'The girls and I handle all the admin and secretarial recruitment. Josh tends to deal with the more technical areas – anything to do with IT or engineering – those are his departments. The boss goes out a lot to the larger companies to meet the HR people, really to make some kind of arrangement for them to forward their search to us. How did you find us?'

'You know *Kinetic Tech* at *Horseshoe Park*? Ed Crane who used to work there is my brother's mate. He told me about the vacant office unit and when I asked about recruitment, mentioned *Accent Recruitment*.'

'How did you come to be with *Accent*?' David continued.

'Goodness me, it's been ages. I came back to live with my mother here when I broke off with my partner about 15 years ago. I had 2 young boys with me and it wasn't easy to find a job. My boss, Jacqui, was kind enough to offer me a part-time job around the hours I had to take the children to school and picking them up. When they were a little older and I could leave them with my mum, I started to work full time.'

'I must admit,' she continued, 'Jacqui had been very good to me. She's someone you can always go to if you have a problem, but somehow she's not somebody you could hang out and have a laugh with. You wouldn't invite her to your children's parties, for instance, if you know what I mean.'

'Is she an older person?'

'Oh Lord yes. She must be in her early sixties, although I can't swear by it.'

Things had turned out better than David had anticipated at Pangbourne. He managed to get a skeleton staff going very quickly with the help of *Accent Recruitment*. The contract on the office lease was signed without a hitch and he managed to rent a small terrace property on Thames Avenue for a year. People were amiable and, after only 3 months, he was recognised at the Bank, the Post Office, the sandwich shops and at several pubs and eating places. When he dropped in at the *Garden Café*, he began to recognise familiar faces. He hoped that after 6 months or so he would not have to come down so often and he could delegate some of the duties to Gavin. It was practical therefore for him to have rented the house for their use. In the long run it would be cheaper and more convenient for them than staying in hotels.

In early July, on a bright sunny morning, he caught a glimpse of her coming out of *NatWest*[1], looking down as she put away her purse into her handbag. He was with Gavin, walking towards the *Copper Inn Hotel*[2] for lunch, but was too far away to ascertain that it was really her. An icy chill coursed through his veins and he had to stop on the bridge over the Pang, pretending to look for fish in the clear stream.

It had been so long ago that he had last thought of her. When they were all together at College, he had known that she was from Reading but had not heard from or about her for way over twenty years. When he turned around again, she was nowhere in view. It

---

[1] NatWest Bank is no longer at Pangbourne
[2] Now called The Elephant

wasn't till the end of the month that he saw her again, in the rain, slightly stooped under an umbrella.

The injustice of it all! She had never told him to his face why she had refused to see him again. All his pleading. The drunken haze through which he lived those last few weeks. The bitterness, the anger, the complete lack of comprehension. The loss of a lover. The loss of the dearest friend. He had vowed never to forgive. And he could picture Michael on the platform, as his train pulled away.

'I can't forgive you. Why are you here?'

'I'll never forgive myself,' Michael had said. David could see his face even then, so many years later. Michael had tried to hug him good-bye. He had pulled himself away.

And now there she was. And he had frozen by the bridge, uncertain of what welcome or antagonism he might receive.

How could he have forgotten to remember them over the years? His own life had turned out well. There was his wife. Then came his children. He had his successful business and circle of friends and family. The past had not intruded. We could all survive the past only to find it of little significance, if only it did not re-visit us to confuse and to confound. He was unsure of his feelings. Their relationship had been short-lived, and he had not dwelt on it for too long since they had parted. There was curiosity about her and what had become of Michael. He walked away. That night he came close to being lonely. The following day he left work early and drove back to the comfort of home.

By early August, his office was fully set up. It was decided between Gavin and him that until more business had started to flow in, he should carry on being in charge at Pangbourne. At some stage in the future, Gavin would spend more time there and leave the running of the Barnet office to his sister, Judy.

One fine Wednesday August afternoon, he rang up Josh to take him out for lunch. Denise was at the reception when he arrived and Josh soon joined them in a lively conversation. They had grown very fond of David's easy and sincere manner. Since he had to pass *Accent Recruitment* on his way to the bank, he occasionally stopped by to say hello to Josh and the girls.

'Oh Jacqui,' Josh called out, as the front door opened, 'this is David Chapman from *Three Points Design and Print*. We have handled his recruitment in the last few months.'

'Hello David,' Jacqueline offered her hand, hesitated momentarily before moving forward to kiss him on both cheeks. 'I'm bowled over. How come we have not bumped into each other before? I'd heard Josh and Denise talk of *Three Points Design and Print*, and of David, but it never occurred to me it would be you. I didn't think this was your part of the world'

'I see you know each other,' Josh laughed. 'It is a small world indeed,' he added.

'Much too many years ago,' Jacqueline said. 'I am so pleased to see you.'

'Josh and I are about to go for lunch,' David said hesitatingly, shocked that he had not connected her with the Jacqui Denise had mentioned, 'would you like to join us?'

'I'm afraid I have a few things to do, but why don't you drop by later?'

Denise had excused herself in the meantime and withdrew to the back office. She had liked David and, in an innocent way, felt possessive of him. They had got on so well, on equal footings. Somehow, with Jacqui on the scene, and David being her friend, she knew their relationship could never be the same again. In a way she had resented that.

She could never understand Jacqui's attraction. How she had landed her husband, whom Denise had considered quite 'dishy', was beyond her. She was not a beautiful woman and was well past her prime, and yet some men seemed to find her engrossing. Denise had noticed that with some of their clients, and it was no better with Josh, who was always so attentive to her.

She respected Jacqui for starting her own business and for the way she had conducted herself in business. Jacqui had taken her on and trained her and had helped her when she had problems with her 2 boys, but somehow they had failed to be two women friends who could confide in each other and laugh and cry together at the same things. She found something lacking in Jacqui – a lack of tenderness and warmth.

After a moment of surprise, Josh did not find it unusual that Jacqui and David could have known each other. She was out and about on business frequently and attended conferences all over the country. However, he saw the look of surprise on her face and the slight bashfulness on David's part. He would deliberate on it a little and then leave it as mere idle curiosity.

David, on the other hand, was pleased that it was Josh and not Denise who was lunching with him. After a casual 'How did you know Jacqui?' from Josh and a brief explanation of College days from him, the matter was laid to rest. Denise would have probed a little further, with enthusiasm and amazement and innuendos. Instead, they had a leisurely lunch on the Thames-side terrace of *The Swan* at Pangbourne. They were both supporters of Arsenal and that offered them sufficient material for an hour's satisfactory conversation.

It had never occurred to Jacqueline that one day David would walk into her life again. He was a brief incident in the past. The incident affected her judgment of future relationship, but he himself was just an occasional memory of a happy and warm episode they had shared with Michael. She was certain that there were times in the last twenty-five years, when both Michael and she, in their togetherness, had sensed a missing element in their life. It was the last piece of the jigsaw that had been misplaced or necessarily left behind with the passing of time. And when it finally turned up again, it would no longer fit meaningfully into the existing matrix, which had faded in intensity and whose edges had been worn from daily attrition and adjustment.

Ever since her last meeting with Gérard, she had been convinced that one should never allow the past to intrude upon the present. Edward had entreated her to seek resolution with Gérard. It was the only way to move forward, he had advised. But Jacqueline knew better now. To get resolution, all sets of cards must be laid open upon the table. But that did not happen in real life. There would always be too many words left unsaid, and too many words said that should have been left unsaid. There could be no resolution in human affairs, only compromises.

The past re-visiting required explanation, required revelation, required avoidance of issues, required balancing and counter-balancing. She reproached herself for such cynicism. After all she was really pleased to see David. They will sort the situation out in no time. She rang Denise to come to her office and to update her on the *Three Points Design and Print* account.

The incessant banging on the door! The desperate call of her name. She covered her head under the pillows and the duvet and they hammered stubbornly still into her resistance. She would not soften. She couldn't let him in. Excuses and explanations - she had had enough of them. Some people had arrived outside her door. There were harsh angry voices. When he had gone she got up and sat on the chair, numb from being a fool, from having assumed that any man could be true. Perhaps she had not been fair to him. She had never expected the affair to continue beyond college. They would go their separate ways. They would find their different lives. But while they were together, she had not dreamed that he would have someone else on the side. Or was she the 'someone' on the side? It was humiliating to be taken in.

She had liked the simplicity in him – the sheer lack of complexity. She had found that restful after all her years with Gérard and after her years in Europe. Her friendship with Michael had been deep and would always be there. She had enjoyed his company most, but their relationship had been an alignment of intellect and of feelings that had never crossed into an embroilment of passion. Michael would always be measured in his moves. David had compensated for that. Together, the three of them had been a unit. David was right. They had been 'in a nutshell'.

There was no necessity now to piece together the shattered past, but she was pleased to see him and she knew Michael would be delighted. They would re-arrange their relationship. There was nothing to forgive. She had been disappointed in him, but everything had turned out as it should. Michael and she were meant to be together. Somewhere in his core Michael had willed it and she had allowed herself to drift effortlessly in its flow. She hoped David was happy.

Josh and David got back just before two. Jacqueline liked that in Josh. He was a principled man and had not taken advantage of being David's guest to be late. And she noticed he had not had a drink. She smiled her approval and led David into her office.

'It's great to see you again, David. There's so much I want to know about you,' she said.

Well, there was so much he wanted to know about her! How could she be so cool, sitting there, smiling, as if nothing traumatic had ever happened between them? Perhaps it was time she told him why she had refused to see him those last weeks at Watford. Why had she dropped him so suddenly, so mercilessly, leaving him desperate and unprepared? Why had she not told him about Michael and her – he might even have understood and stepped aside. He felt she owed him an explanation.

'We can't talk here,' she added. 'Why don't we go for a walk? Have you been down to Thames Meadows? Let's go there,' she suggested.

They stopped by at *Wilflower*, the greengrocer's[1], where she bought a few plums, and then next door at *Green's*, the butcher's.

'Hi Phil, have you any hot pie? Oh, the chicken curry would do, as long as it is hot. Hi Sue,' she said as

---

[1] Wilflower no longer exists but the premises are now part of Green's

she turned to pay at the cash counter. 'I haven't had time to have lunch yet,' she explained to David.

Thames Meadows was a long stretch of grassy bank along the Thames. This was a typical *The Wind in The Willow* country. On its left is the toll bridge across from Pangbourne in Berkshire to Whitchurch in Oxfordshire. A few boats were moored there that quiet weekday afternoon. Some mallards, a pair of coots and a lone swan resting near the bank began to stir in anticipation of being fed when David and Jacqueline approached one of the bank-side benches.

'So tell me about yourself, David.'

What an all-encompassing, impossible question to answer, David thought. 'Where could I start?' he asked.

'Have you a family?' she enquired.

'Well, Susan my wife and I met at a mutual friend's wedding. We got married and have 2 children. Gavin the elder boy comes down to Pangbourne sometimes and Judy, my daughter, looks after our Barnet office for me. Susan is a teacher.'

'Susan? So you did not marry Gloria,' Jacqueline enquired, slightly surprised.

'Gloria? Which Gloria?' asked a perplexed David.

'The Gloria at Watford. I saw you together at the park. Oh! David, how you men forget the women in your life!' Jacqueline laughed.

'Forgotten? You think I had forgotten you?' David protested. In his heart he knew that there was some truth in what Jacqueline had said. He had got on with his life and over the years Jacqueline had become a non-issue.

'Gloria was nothing,' he continued, 'just a brief relationship I had. I didn't know you knew about her. Why didn't you ask me about her if you had seen her? Or, at least, ask Michael? He knew it was all over between us. That was why she was there. She had insisted on going to meet me after I had broken up with her. Michael knew that. Is that why you..? I never understood why you refused to see me. How do you think I felt? To lose you and then to lose Michael without an explanation? I blamed Michael for taking you away from me and he had never disputed that.'

'Oh, David, I am so, so sorry. I'd no idea. Seeing you together, she in your arms, I thought you were cheating on me. Of course I knew men cheated. I was done with excuses and explanations, and I didn't want any of that. I was angry with you and didn't want to be further humiliated. However, it wasn't as a lover that you had hurt me, it was as a friend. A friend wouldn't cheat. He would be honest. He would put me in the picture. And so all these years I thought you had done me an injustice. Oh, David, I am so sorry.'

'You could have asked me. Didn't you realise that for the first time in my life I really thought I loved somebody in a grown up way? You and Michael and I, together, all destroyed because you didn't have the decency to ask me about it.'

'I didn't know. I didn't know. It is inexcusable, David, but, thinking what I did, I had forgiven you, so please forgive me. Not for now, but for the misunderstanding then. You are happy now, with a family. Perhaps we should be grateful for that.'

'And what about Michael? Are you together?'

'Yes. We were married in 81. You know Michael – always the slow worker, but it had worked out well. Look, David, we were never really suited to each other. We're so different. Both Michael and I thought the world of you. Please don't mention what we had discussed just now to him. You know him. He could be so sensitive and start questioning and blaming himself. You will come and see him won't you? Why don't you come on Friday, for supper?'

'I can't make it this Friday.'

'Next Friday then. He would be so thrilled when I tell him.'

'I've seen you several times in the village,' David volunteered.

'And you didn't stop me to say hello? You must have hated me, David.'

'I was confused. It had been so long and I wasn't sure how you would react. Perhaps I thought it was best to leave well alone.'

'I'm glad we have met. I must get back to the office. You will come Friday week, won't you? Come early. Michael could get the afternoon off.'

'I'll walk you back,' David said, 'I have to see Josh about some CVs.' As an after-thought, he said, 'you haven't touched your lunch.'

David looked at her. She must be in her sixties. A sudden blush of embarrassment took hold of him. What could he have seen in her? She was so much older than he was and so plain. Not the sort of woman he fancied. If there had been feelings, they had been forgotten. It was finished business, which did not warrant analysis. He would love to see Michael again. If there had been no Michael there would have been no Jacqueline in his life. Somehow, at Watford, he had been drawn tighter and tighter into a vortex of emotion and of needs whose axis swung between Michael and Jacqueline.

Back at her office, Jacqueline tried to reach Michael unsuccessfully. She was excited for him. There were times when she had felt responsible for breaking up his friendship with David. Friendship, she held sacred. Love could come and go. It could take on so many guises and be as ephemeral as the urgent flights of May Flies winging into the sky. When it was fortunate enough to endure, it endured within the bower of friendship. So she felt as if she were returning something precious to her husband.

Why, it was almost like a homecoming.

Something David had said niggled her, but she pushed it to the back of her mind. 'Michael knew about it', he had said more than once. She would not think about that right away. She refused to ask relevant questions. It was a happy occasion to have him back in their lives. She would prepare a meal for them, and if she could persuade him to stay the night, she would get in plenty of beer for him. If the weather held fine, they could sit on the balcony outside their bedroom and drink and chat into the early hours. Like old time. Perhaps Michael would strum on his guitar.

The phone rang. She turned slightly and picked it up.

It was almost a quarter to 8 before Michael got in that evening. He put away his briefcase in the study before going into the kitchen.

'Darling,' he said as he gave Jacqueline a light kiss. 'I've got your message about David.'

'Could you imagine him turning up at Pangbourne? It gave me quite a turn when I saw him at my office.'

'Are you OK about it?'

'Yes,' she frowned. 'He explained things. I suppose I'd got the wrong end of the stick at Watford. We can talk about it some other time. I've invited him to dinner for Friday week. He couldn't make it this Friday. You could get back early couldn't you?'

'Sure, it'd be good to see him again. Is he OK?'

'Oh yes. The same old David. A little rounder around the waist. You look tired. I have a quiche in the oven – another 10 minutes.' She looked at him again and added, 'He would want to see you, you know.'

He did feel rather tired. A distant rumble of fear appeared to have drained him of energy. He questioned the grounds on which he had built his love, his marriage, his future. Would the equilibrium they had maintained without David begin to shift with his return?

He had no concern regarding Jacqueline's feelings towards David. He had never regarded them as a grand passion on Jacqueline's part. Her reaction to David was one of anger and disappointment and of hurt pride. She and David could never have worked it out. He knew. His fears lay not in David but in himself. It brought forth questions of what Jacqueline and he represented to each other. His integrity – her trust. The mileage that had passed and that which was to come. He felt threats, churning, churning threats.

That summer of 77. David had wanted to get even drunker. He had wanted to get drunk with David. They sat in a corner on their own at the *Coach Maker*, biding time but getting drunk. For once, David was quiet. Twice somebody had tried to join them, but Michael had simply held up his hand and shook his head slightly. David, through bleary eyes, wanted to know, slurringly, why Jacqueline had, all of a sudden, refused to see him. The question was rhetorical. He did not expect Michael to know the answer.

He did not know that a few days before, while walking through Cassiobury Park, Jacqueline and Michael had approached the River Gad and, looking across to the humpback bridge over the Grand Union Canal, they had come upon him and Gloria in an embrace. Michael could see them still, with David's head resting on hers, oblivious to all around them. He had known that they would be there but had feigned to turn Jacqueline around. She had already noticed them. Without saying a word, she turned and walked away.

From that afternoon, Jacqueline had refused to see or talk to David. Michael understood perfectly her reasoning. He tried as much as possible to support David. He listened to him. He drank with him. He stressed the importance of his studies. He tried to make him see that there was only just over a month before they would leave college and that his life would happen all over again with someone more suitable. He was surprised at how inconsolable David was. He had not expected such tenacity in David's feelings.

All the burden of the situation began to fall on his shoulders. The treacherous part he had played and the hypocrisy tinged with sincere affection drove him to put his arms around David to comfort him but, simultaneously, it filled him with self-revulsion. It was after all about his survival – but at what price, with what sacrifice? He had to get drunk in order to bear the weight in his heart.

It was almost 11 at night but the sky still had a midsummer glow beyond the darkness of the trees. They had made their way deep into Cassiobury Park with a six pack of lager. Under a shrouding old beech tree they sat cross-legged, each with a can of lager. David took a small pouch out of his trouser pocket and passed it on to Michael together with a pack of Rizla. Michael loosened the weed gently and lifted a good pinch to put on the paper. He licked an edge of the paper, carefully rolled it, giving the end a twist before lighting it and passing it to David.

He lay on the grass with eyes closed. He felt demeaned and cowardly for resorting to drink and drug to gain some courage to stab his much loved friend, already trodden, already broken, in the back. All his principles shed like a superficial coat, baring his flaws, showing him up as worse than other men. And from that day on he would have to live with that knowledge.

All these for a woman? He knew even as he thought it that that was not so. It was all for his own survival. He was careless of her happiness or of David's. He was careless even of his own possible happiness, for that was still debatable. In his frailty, he could not allow her to go out of his life. It was an opportunity that had arisen and he had merely kept silent on what he knew.

How honed was the edge of 'merely'.

'Here,' David muttered, passing the joint to him.

He sat up and drew it in deeply, his eyes brimming with tears, as he explained to David that Jacqueline and he were lovers and that it was why she would not see him and that she could not bear to tell him the truth.

'I'm so sorry, David, I'm so sorry,' he said, and seeing David, distraught and unbelieving, he wept.

Jacqueline decided on something simple for dinner – something hearty and well-tried which would not keep her too much in the kitchen. Something meaty which she thought would suit David. She bought some thick-end of beef skirt from *Green's*. Then she went to the wine shop to get a bottle of young, red burgundy – Michael had once mentioned that it was suitable for a boeuf Bourguignon. She would serve this with some boiled potatoes and beans. For dessert she had bought a tarte au citron from *Waitrose*[1]. That, she told herself, would be good enough for a casual meal.

The meal shouldn't take her more than an hour and a half to get ready. She would only start on it when David had arrived. She must ensure that Michael and David had some time on their own. She was convinced that they had issues to sort out too.

From the kitchen window she could see David arriving just past 5 o'clock in his white Mercedes E Class. Michael was tinkering with his Yamaha outside the garage. Looking up as David's car crunched its way onto the pebbled drive, Michael was not surprised to see him in a Mercedes. As he manoeuvred his car towards the edge of the drive, David could see Jacqueline's red Citroen 2CV in the garage. Beside it was a black Volkswagen Golf that he presumed belonged to Michael.

Whilst driving a Mercedes was an aspiration to him, a sign of social and financial success, David was rather peeved that people like Michael never had to prove themselves, being recognised as middle class and even money-classed, without needing to flaunt their wealth, which they may or may not actually have. While they

---

[1] A supermarket chain

were at Watford, he had not felt this distinction so keenly, having been so close to both of them. He had done very well for himself and considered himself a rich man, but still felt he had something to prove.

He was pleasantly surprised to see Michael's Yamaha, still gleaming and in good condition. Michael came to the car and gave David a big hug as he got out, for which David was grateful. He had been debating as to how to greet Michael again after all that had passed between them and after such a long time.

'Did you find us easily?' Jacqueline enquired when they joined her in the kitchen. She was arranging some apples and clementines in a large fruit bowl. The informality of being taken to the kitchen rather than into the sitting room, made David feel more at ease. She offered David a can of lager from the fridge and a glass and ushered them towards the sitting room. Michael declined a lager for himself.

'I thought I'll take David for a spin on my bike while you prepare dinner,' Michael said. 'There's no hurry David, after the beer.'

There was nothing pretentious about the house, David thought. The kitchen was small and dated and the house itself was smaller than it first appeared to be. It was long and narrow with the length itself presented as the frontage. The lounge was of a fair size with a very large picture window on the front opening onto the wide garden. While standing, David could just see beyond the tall hedge towards the first rise of the Chilterns above the valley of the Thames.

He was subconsciously comparing this house with his own and came to the conclusion that, except for the location, he owned a superior property. His trend of thought was interrupted when Jacqueline came in with the bowl of fruit with a few bananas added to it and placed it on the coffee table, wondering if David would like to have some before going off with Michael. David stretched out to pick up a clementine, hesitated, decided against it and chose a banana instead.

The room was comfortable enough. It leaned towards cosiness. There was the large sofa, some years old, with its seats shabby with use. The scatter cushions, and there were many of them, were not all matching or plumped up. The two main chairs had seen better days. David could imagine Michael and Jacqueline sitting like an old couple each evening, doing whatever boring thing they might, like listening to classical music or reading books, or watching the news. It was not a room for entertaining. In a way he was disappointed with Michael. It was not the way he had expected of him. When he thought of Michael, he thought of grace, of good taste, of class. But then what did he know of Michael? As for Jacqueline, there was always a quirkiness about her, something almost foreign, perhaps European. He did not expect of her regulation, or sensible British orderliness.

He felt fortunate that Susan had a very feminine and discriminating eye for décor. The furnishing in the house was of the best and there was order and cleanliness. The rooms always felt fresh, ready for entertaining or for guests who needed to stay. You knew that much care and taste had gone into their creation.

What a lucky escape he had had. Jacqueline wouldn't have been right for him. Again he felt slightly embarrassed by the thought of his past ardour. Michael could have told him years ago that it would be a misalliance.

Corner Oak stood at the junction of two narrow lanes, surrounded by leafy acreages and open fields of neighbouring properties and a National Trust Park with its imposing house. Situated on the brow of the foothills of the Berkshire Downs, it had a picture postcard view of the valley of the Thames and the Chilterns beyond it. Built in the sixties in what was once a corner of a neighbour's garden, the modest house was further humbled by the larger and older character houses around it. Close to where the two lanes met, stood a single, old oak tree, giving rise to the name of the property.

Michael rode his bike uphill through the village along windy lanes and then down towards the A329 Reading Road and into Streatley. From Streatley, he took the Rectory road which led to the *Ridgeway* which in turn graced its way towards *Bury Down*.

David was not familiar with rural England. He was by nature a city person and on holidays would head for the crowded seaside resorts in the Mediterranean or the Spanish islands. The deeply rutted *Ridgeway* meant a bumpy ride even though Michael swerved and tried to avoid the deeper grooves as much as he could. David could not see the point of it all. He would have preferred a well maintained road. However, it reminded him of their holiday in France a long time ago. It brought back to him their comradeship, their youth and their one-time solid friendship.

His life in between, his marriage, his family, his success in business and his current social circle, became a discrete entity, quite irrelevant to the present dynamic between Michael, Jacqueline and him. He still felt deeply hurt by Michael's confession and betrayal before the end of their time at Watford that he was in a relationship with Jacqueline. At that time he had considered it disloyal and unpardonable. Once again now, he felt he was at the centre of some insidious, fateful manipulation beyond his grasp. It would have been wise for him to walk away from it all, but he was drawn towards them.

When he met Jacqueline again, he knew he was safe. There was no emotional agitation of any kind. He had seen nothing remotely worth pursuing in her. But when he saw Michael and her together, when he saw the way Michael looked at her, when he heard them talking, he realised that there must be some underlying traits in her which sustained their relationship. Surely he must have been affected by them too during those Watford days for the pain to be so bitter when she left him.

Michael tapped him lightly on his arm with his fist. 'Alright?' he asked.

'Alright' in what way? David thought. Alright with the past? Alright with being back together with him and Jacqueline? Alright as being in good health? Alright being confused with new equivocal bits of information? No, he was not alright. Perhaps getting together again was a bad idea. They were both grown men now. Unless they were to drag the past into the present, they had nothing in common any longer. There was no room for new binding emotions.

'I'm good,' he replied, looking down across the farms and villages of south Oxfordshire. He was surprised at how much more uncomfortable he was with Michael than with Jacqueline. During their days at Watford, he had always looked up to Michael as the one who knew what was what. Facing him now in the middle of nowhere, David resented the renaissance of this deference towards him.

'Come, let's get back,' Michael said, seeing that David was sneezing. 'You didn't use to suffer from hay fever, did you?' he asked.

'Not that I could remember, but it's all these fields here which must have triggered it off.'

He noticed how short Michael wore his hair now. A little grey at the temples had added gravity to his appearance. Whenever David had remembered him, it was of the freshness of youth, of the quiet enthusiasm for the future, of the subtle and suppleness of mind. He now appeared so much more mature in look and in demeanour. Even more taciturn, but still the sensible Michael he had known.

Over the years, David had put on a little weight and lost a little weight depending on the calendar. Christmas, birthdays, anniversaries and holidays were times of indulgence to be followed by periods of restraint. In recent years, coaxed by Susan, he had joined a health club. Although he had kept his weight in check, it was almost impossible for him to lose the noticeable paunch. He liked to laugh it off as a sign of success and a good life.

He now looked enviously at Michael, who might play a few games of tennis in a month and who had probably never seen the inside of a gym, but had retained a youthful fitness and trimness.

'Come,' Michael said, 'don't let's keep Jacqueline waiting.'

'Why don't you take David up to the balcony?' Jacqueline suggested after dinner. 'I'll clear the table and prepare some coffee.'

The balcony could be reached up a flight of cast iron steps from the outside or directly from the main bedroom. Michael took David through the latter onto this large, stone paved area which ran the width of the bedroom and extended past it over the study below. It had the same but uninterrupted view over the Thames valley that David had seen from the sitting room.

In a corner was a careless arrangement of tubs of bushy bamboo, a red maple that had reverted to green and some petunias. David couldn't help thinking of what pristine, catalogue cover marvel Susan might have made of such a space.

They sat at a small round aluminium table on aluminium chairs. Susan would have gone for wood, probably teak or oak. Aluminium outdoor furniture suggested some pavement outside a café or pub in the centre of town.

'Are you in touch with anyone from College?' Michael enquired.

'No, no one. I ran into Dickie about 2 years' ago in London. He worked with a marketing company in Derby. We had a drink together. He still kept in touch with Natalie. What about you?'

'Only with Clinger. She came to see us in 96 and we went over to see her two years ago.'

'She's OK? Where is she?'

'Oh yes. I think she is enviously happy. She's married with 4 children and they live in Tasmania – in a small dairy farm. Yes, life suits her fine. She always wanted children. Lovely kids too. I think Jacqueline was quite taken with their life-style,' Michael confided. 'Clinger always had a simple outlook on life – someone to love and lots of children. Sometimes we make our life too complex,' he added. 'We both like her husband, Don, a lot.'

Jacqueline came through the bedroom with the coffee tray. She placed the large bone china cafetière and the white, fluted Wedgwood Candlelight china on the table. She had not forgotten that David took milk and sugar. From the bedroom she brought out a large, bulbous, glass goblet, weighted down slightly by fine white sand on which rested a lit stout candle – a gift from Denise a couple of Christmases ago. On the way back to the house, she switched on the balcony wall light and went to look for the box of dark chocolates in the kitchen. She tidied up the kitchen, giving Michael and David plenty of time together, before joining them again.

Michael was strumming *Moon River* on his guitar and smiled at her when she got back. He knew she loved it when they had some quiet time together and he played the guitar. They had decided a long time ago that a piano was too ostentatious for a small house like theirs, but he had not found it too much of a sacrifice.

David noticed that smile from Michael which lingered as Jacqueline poured some coffee for both of them. It was a smile which intrigued him. He could not remember ever smiling that way or seeing Susan smiled that way at him. It was a meagre smile, but one that was so comprehensive of feelings to someone sensitive to its reception. He was certain Jacqueline was. And in a strange third party way he was receptive to it.

It was a quiet way of expressing feelings. It was a quiet way of spending an evening. Except for the occasional rumbling of a distant train in the valley and the rare passing of a car, the gentle strumming of the guitar was the only clear, precise sound in the night.

When David and Susan had guests, or when the children were at home, there was always laughter, music or the television, hearty conversations and activities which drowned out thoughts. Here one was keen to the silence and to the stars on that cloudless night. One was sensitive to each other's presence and Michael's gentle strumming carried them almost to that other end of the rainbow. David was touched and allowed himself to be enveloped within this new experience.

He could not tell whether Michael was happy, but he knew that after so many years of being together, Michael was still in love with Jacqueline. In so many vague and unexplainable ways, he was disappointed with Michael. He had always presumed that Michael would be exceptionally successful in his career and be a social or public figure. There was nobody he had esteemed or a friend he had loved as much.

'Some women,' he thought, 'are the catalyst, the propelling force, the inspiration and the support towards a man's success. Others, like Jacqueline, are the end of an aspiration itself.' He could not help thinking what Michael might have become with the right woman by his side.

'Disappointment,' she spitted out, 'that's the only word I have for you.'

Michael looked away from his mother. He had not expected her to understand. There was no way of explaining to her what he himself had not understood.

He knew and that was good enough for him. He felt detached from the conversation which was all about him. He could not feel involved with what she had to say. He was not angry with her. It was all just so unnecessary.

'You were a brilliant student when you were at school. See where you are now.'

'I was not brilliant,' Michael insisted.

'Brilliant!' his mother reiterated. 'Mr Bradman used to tell me he had great expectation of you. I could understand that you might want to be rebellious. Lots of children are. But I would have expected you to rebel but in a self-improving way.'

'That would be self-defeating, don't you think, mother?'

She straightened in her chair, gripping the arms to control herself. When Michael started to call her mother instead of mum, it irritated her. She knew he was putting a barrier between them.

'And now you come up with this rubbish about marrying that horrid woman,' she attacked from a different angle.

'You know her so well, do you mother?' Michael said, remaining calm.

'I disliked her from the first time I met her,' she retorted. 'Your father wasn't enamoured with her either. When I think that all your cousins on both my side and your father's are so sensible and doing so well, it fills me with shame. They are no more intelligent than you are. And what are you going to do a few years down the line? When you are 30 she'll be whatever age she would be, so much older. You think you will be happy then? Then what? Stay on and be miserable?'

'I'll deal with that problem when I come to it. For all you know, you might be lucky and things will work out right.'

'And if it didn't? You have dismissed any kind of sensible careers and would break up your family as well?'

'God-willing, mother, there might not be a family.'

'There is really no use talking to you Michael. I'll wash my hands of you. You wait till your dad hears of this.'

'Dad would have nothing to say that you have not already said. Anyway I will need to go. The date is October 12th. I'll send you an invitation,' Michael said, as he rose to go.

'You needn't bother. We won't be there.'

'Well, you are welcome if you changed your mind. There'll only be Jacqueline and me and a couple of friends as witnesses.'

'Of course she was not wrong in principles,' Michael thought. 'When we pass judgment we are seldom wrong in principles, but are almost always wrong with regards to the person we pass the judgment on.' Standing on the balcony looking out and down the valley, he felt there had only ever been one path he would take. The right or wrong of it had never been an issue.

He had had his dreams. In his early teens he came across Arthur Grimble's *A Pattern of Islands* about life in the Gilbert and Ellice islands[1] in the West-Central Pacific. He then discovered Somerset Maugham and his tales of the South Seas[2]. His fascination began. Not for him the life of a professional or a successful business man. He knew he would finish college, find himself a job, saved some money and then drift towards these far off islands. He could see the white coral sand edging the islands, feel the balmy breeze stirring among the coconut palms, look up towards the cloud-clad mountains and imagine swimming in clear, cool mountain pools. He would go native and casually drape a colourful hand-printed pareo around his waist and drape his arms around the nubile brown bodies of beautiful islanders with flowing long, black hair. Oh, the perfume from the exotic flowers in their hair.

He realised that he was a dreamer and a romantic at heart. Like his Maugham hero, Edward Barnard[3], he would lead a simple life in a simple hut among coconut palms and have a lovely, uncomplicated girl by his side. Marriage was not a participating element in his dream. He would then drift on towards some other

---

[1] Now known as Tuvalu

[2] Oceania

[3] Somerset Maugham: The Fall of Edward Barnard – a short story within 'The Trembling of a Leaf'

island and fall in love again and perhaps have his heart broken several times.

Or, like Larry Darrell in *The Razor's Edge*, he would give up love and creature comfort and travel to India in search of something mystical.

When he had grown weary of all these, if he had not intellectually or emotionally found his niche, he would then return to England and settle down to a job. He would consider himself a man already endowed with the riches of experience and freedom.

When he decided he must have Jacqueline in his life, he knew it was the end of his youthful dreams. He had to allow some convention to guide his future, although Jacqueline was not exactly a conventional person. He had not, from the very start, considered it a sacrifice. Sacrifice meant giving up something of value for something of a lesser value. In his craving for Jacqueline to be a part of his life, he believed that it was a fair exchange.

Reality could be an even greater adventure. It was a greater unknown than lands already discovered and life already led, albeit vicariously. Life would be trickier and a little darker with Jacqueline than among the assumed innocence of the islanders. Of course Michael realised, even before he had met Jacqueline, that the world had changed rapidly and that if he were to go there now, the South Sea and Pacific Islands could only be a dreary disappointment. He could not bear to shatter his enchantment with the world of Grimble and Maugham.

The light went off in David's room. The sky gained depth from the sudden darkness and the stars twinkled in clear, sharp points. Michael could not see Orion – it was perhaps too late in the night. He slid shut the balcony door behind him and, stripping down to his boxer shorts, he lay down on the duvet, next to Jacqueline. In spite of the clear sky, the night was humid. She was lying on her side facing away from him. He gently put his hand on the rise of her hip and let it rest there without waking her. It was unlikely that he would fall asleep any time soon. He was certain that David was fast asleep.

Happiness was over-rated – the tedium of knowing that it was always there, unchangingly pleasant, monotonous. He preferred to catch glimpses of it – the elusive devil. He preferred to be momentarily enthralled by it and then to miss it terribly, once again desirous of it.

There were rare moments of pure bliss when he had looked into Jacqueline's eyes and recognised that 'conjunction' of the mind [1]. Then he knew they belonged. Then he had felt safe. In those moments she had opened up, softened, put her disillusionment with men aside and found him. They could have just been to the theatre, or listened to a piece of music, or said something, and then looked at each other and that depth of feeling arose and bound them.

---

[1] Andrew Marvell: The Definition of Love

He looked at love making this way. In its intensity, its bursting pleasure, its togetherness of giving and taking, it was but the call of nature. Other beings felt the same, even though each might have been convinced that he had experienced that peak of sensation nobody else could have attained. He was not singled out to be its champion. He had to accept too that with all her experience, Jacqueline might have found it a jaded pleasure from the very start. Somewhere along the line it might have become blasé. He could never be able to bring to her that freshness of discovery of first loves, but he was not unsatisfied.

He was under no delusion that if time could be shifted and they had met when both were young, that they would have been attracted to each other. She would not have been the Jacqueline that he now loved, with the punch of self-assurance, the wells of knowledge, the slight cynicism in her manner and the acceptance that we were all faulty beings.

And a faulty being he had been.

Jacqueline turned around, stretching to hold him, but finding that he was lying on the duvet instead of under it, she rolled over again. Michael pulled the duvet up on his side and then rolled over to get under its cover. He moulded his body to hers as best he could and softly kissed her on the shoulder.

And a faulty being he had been – he resumed his thoughts.

Maria de Souza, five foot seven, tall for an Asian woman. Her long, wavy, black hair gleamed healthily in the sun or in any other light. Skin – Mediterranean, but lightened for being kept from the sun. Beautiful as only several generations of mixed racial marriages could produce. On her father's side she had acquired the dusky skin tone and strong black hair of the Portuguese; the delicate frame with a slender waistline of the Chinese; the dark thick lashes of the Southern Indians. From her mother's side came the slightly haughty bearing of the English; the long, slim arms without the least bit of flap, so typical of the Chinese in their youth, and the long, arched neck, that could be traced back to some dubious Dutch merchant seaman.

What men found most appealing about her, after the initial double-take of her physical beauty, was the confidence, the openness, the intelligence, the chic and her facility with the English language. She was interesting company. What would have been a stigma fifty years earlier, her mixed origin now made her both exotic and arresting from so many angles.

They had met the year before at a trade fair in Hong Kong. His company had purchased several electronic parts from Hai Chung Electronics in Guangzhou in the past. As an honoured guest he was assigned the company of Maria, their marketing manager in Hong Kong. Originally from Macau, she spoke fluent English, could curse bitchily in Cantonese and spit out some offensive asides in Portuguese. She had organised the dinners and the meetings and accompanied him on a factory visit in Guangzhou.

It was his last day in Hong Kong. After a sumptuous dim sum lunch amidst ornate, gold, red, blue and green carved dragons and phoenixes and the noisiest crowd of businessmen, Michael and Maria returned to the Excelsior hotel on the sea-front. They settled down for a drink at the bar. What Michael wanted was to get back to his room and have a rest before the rigmarole of going out to dinner with the same people from Hai Chung again. However, Maria had other things on her mind. She invited him up to her room for coffee.

At 26 years of age, she was not ready to settle down. She intended to do well for herself in the business world, save some money in case of rainy days, before seriously looking out for a prospective husband. And he had to be a prospect. Her standards required a husband to be rich and successful, to have a certain level of education and standing in society and to have the stamina to continue to be so.

She had no delusions about love and romance. A rich and successful man would always expect a trophy wife whom he could display in public, who could entertain his friends and clients in and outside the home, who would eventually provide him with a family. She was perfectly qualified for all that. Eventually, she would not be surprised if he was to look elsewhere for younger and shinier trophies, but she would have been established as his wife and the mother of his children. As long as she was clever enough and played her cards wisely, he might stray but she would remain the hub of the family. There was nothing more pliable than a guilty husband as long as she was willing to play the ever-loving but long suffering wife. Love and romance would only get in the way of a stable marriage.

In the meantime, she had fun, but she was discreet. Her reputation must not be tarnished. She found Michael very attractive. He was a foreigner who had come and would then be gone. She liked his charming ways and the way he spoke. He could be trusted with her indiscretion.

Maria was not someone Michael would know how to say no to. He felt that when a woman was beautiful, intelligent and capable, it must be so much more painful to be rejected than if she were plain. Rejection was something unfamiliar to her. She would be furious and embarrassed and indignant that she had been found wanting. There would be nothing of the humility and modesty of a plainer woman to aid her understanding of the situation. So Michael, with civility, complied with her advances.

The whole episode was summed up very neatly by Maria as – unremarkable. Not worth the trouble. She had offered up a voluptuous feast and he had dipped in for a canapé. But she would have been appalled to discover the insignificance to which Michael had attached the incident. To him, it was inconsequential. It was like nibbling at a snack when he felt peckish, or spilling some wine on his shirt during lunch, or winning a casual game of squash. It was of so little matter that he had not even stopped to feel guilty about it towards Jacqueline. Such events he considered as the incidentals to a relationship, to a marriage. As long as the core is sound, these would become dead twigs which one could brush off without dire consequences.

When he returned to Hong Kong 3 years later, Maria had moved on, and he found the presence of Edwin Lee so much more businesslike and uncomplicated.

It had not occurred to Michael to tell Jacqueline of this incident. At the back of his mind he knew that Jacqueline would probably have shrugged her shoulders and rapped him on the knuckles. She was too worldly to have given much weight to it. However, as he lay beside her, he realised that one day soon, he would have to sit down with her and explain to her his role in her break-up with David.

He knew he was in the wrong. He knew his deviousness should be unforgivable. He did not expect Jacqueline to forgive him. He could envisage the dry chill that would pervade their world together afterwards – a dry chill in which no tenderness, no anger and no love could survive. But he knew she would still remain from a sense of duty. Because he cared, he would find the situation unbearable.

He rolled on his side away from Jacqueline and with his eyes wide open, he considered how he might survive. He knew that the core, so important in the thread of his argument of stability, was a core of rotten lies, so long lying dormant, and was about to erupt and spume its paths of destruction. Until that time came, he wanted to savour the softness of lying beside her in apparent innocence.

The blackbirds, tits, finches, thrushes and robins at the bird feeders and the occasional cooing of wood pigeons woke David early the next morning. Damn nuisance, he fumed. Why would anyone want to live in the country, he marvelled.

Facing him as he sat up in bed was a framed Degas reproduction of ballet dancers. It was not a large picture, about an A3[1]. There were small groups of dancers on stage with one sitting on a bench. He found it insipid. Imagine a monochrome of sepia on White in a bedroom equally devoid of warm colours! He was once again disappointed with how colourless his friends had become.

He went quietly downstairs. Jacqueline was already in the kitchen preparing coffee, toasts and croissants. She persuaded him to sit down to a light breakfast and wait for Michael, who was already up. Michael would be disappointed not to see him before he went. David noticed that there was not sufficient space in the kitchen for a casual table. Susan and he hardly ever used the dining table unless they had guests. During the day, the kitchen was the hub of their family life

---

[1] 29.7cm x 42.0cm or 11.692 x 16.53"

when the children were living at home and had remained to be so.

They sat down at the dining table, both reaching for their coffee, for a moment not having anything to say. It gave David enough time to take in an impression of her. No doubt she was elegant. He thought of her in term of the vertical rather than the horizontal or the curvy. Her arms, her body, her neck were just so slightly extended, lending a certain amount of '*Greco*'[1] grace to her, whether in movement or being still. Personally, he was more comfortable, felt more assured, with women who exuded more warmth and easy laughter. Someone more forthcoming with light conversation. Someone more femininely rounded than angular. Someone more like Susan than Jacqueline.

He couldn't wait to drive home. His daughter would be there and together with Susan, they would go and do their weekly shopping in the afternoon. In the evening they would be meeting up at the pub with Gavin and his girlfriend, and it would be fun. The following Bank Holiday weekend, they had invited family and friends over for a barbecue and that, he knew, would carry on till the early hours of the morning. There would be noise, laughter, movement and society.

He thought – these were silhouette figures, Michael and Jacqueline, living mono-dimensional lives. Then Michael joined them, helped himself to a cup of black

---

[1] Reference to El Greco the artist

coffee, touched Jacqueline briefly on the shoulder before sitting down, and an inundation of memories filled David of those days when he had been a part of them. Those days when he too had been happy, when his heart was full, when he had needed no one and nothing else besides.

The unexpected revelation that the secret of silhouettes was that you have to be on the other side with the light and the clarity of vision pained him immeasurably. Silhouettes are the unreality of the beholder and his sad lack of imagination and penetration. He knew of a sudden that what he was soon going to leave behind weighed more desirously than what he had only a moment ago, rightly, been eagerly reaching home for.

While Jacqueline went to the kitchen to fetch more coffee, Michael took the opportunity to enquire after David's parents whom he had met several times but Jacqueline had not. Their welcome and warmth towards him the few times he had stayed over with them had left an indelible impression on him.

He had envied David the open, loud and non-cerebral relationship he had with his parents and his brother and sister. That so much affection and so much expression of it should come so naturally, to be so much taken for granted, was quite alien to him and his family. They were uptight people. They had to consider and weigh before they could express. Having considered and weighed, they were therefore less capable of accepting a difference of opinion. They each had to be discrete in their own belief, unable to be within the simple embrace of warm, friendly or familial togetherness.

'Mum and Dad live with Tony now. He had an annexe built for them to one side of the house. Mum is still going strong, a little arthritic, but Dad is almost housebound these days. He suffers from diabetes and is overweight.'

'It's wonderful of Tony to have them stay with him. Does your Jean live nearby still?'

'Oh yes, she sees my parents every day. She was divorced some years ago and is now re-married. Fortunately for mum and dad, she is retired and has more time for them than Tony or Janet.'

He accepted another mug of coffee from Jacqueline and, turning back to Michael asked about his parents.

'My mother died 6 years ago, which was a shock to all of us. We always thought she was the one who would outlast everybody else. My father lives in Germany now with his German wife. She has 3 children of her own and they are much more a family to my dad than I am or ever will be. So, we don't really see much of each other.'

'Why don't both of you come over to us on Bank Holiday Sunday? We are having a barbecue at my place and the whole clan will be there. Mum and Dad would love to see you again, Michael,' David suggested.

'That would be wonderful,' Jacqueline replied, pouring out coffee for David, 'but, unfortunately, we will be in France that weekend. We try to get away on Bank Holidays whenever possible.'

'Perhaps some other time,' Michael added, 'I would love to see your family again. Send my love to your parents and Tony and Jean.'

The old 2CV had had its day of being driven all over France, from Normandy and Brittany to the Loire and the Dordogne; from Champagne and Burgundy to Chamonix. It had had its glory days. The chassis had rusted and the clutch was not always reliable, so its enjoyment was restricted to England and Wales. They crossed the Channel Tunnel very early in their Golf, avoiding the busy Bank Holiday Ferry crossings.

Outside of school holidays, they would have taken a ferry. They loved the feel of the breeze, which also brought the smell of the salty sea to them. It recalled to Jacqueline the many trips she used to make when she was younger. As for Michael, deep inside, there still lurked the romance of the high seas. Harbour lights, fog horns, screeching gulls, the next shore, all vaguely moved him. But they would avoid the overcrowding and the oppressive noise made by holiday-makers.

Arriving too early for lunch, they drove to *Auchan*[1] at the far side of Calais to do their shopping before continuing on to St Omer about 40km away. This was their usual stop on short trips into France. Large enough for the type of shops they liked but still

---

[1] A French Supermarket chain

unspoilt with overdevelopment, St Omer was close to Calais and yet was a world apart. The English travellers who made it there, and they did, as the number of bars bearing English names would testify, were perhaps a little more sedate, a little less out for a jolly good time. They were there for a short break, for the food and the drinking at La Place du Maréchal Foch, and for the Saturday market or they were on their way somewhere else. They might stroll to the Aa[1] or into the park by the town, or venture out to the crystal factory at Arques[2]. It was by far an adult place where relationship could be discreetly started or gently renewed.

It had continued to rain from Calais to St Omer. They always stayed at a town centre hotel so that they could both drink and walk to the restaurants. Having failed to book a room at *Les Frangins*, they settled for the *Ibis Hotel* just off La Place du Maréchal Foch. Their room, on the third floor, opened out to the narrow street at the side of the hotel, facing tall shuttered windows of apartments.

They unpacked their shopping from *Auchan* – oysters, whelks, crevettes, rich mayonnaise, a lemon, baguettes and a couple of bottles of Chablis. Like an often repeated ritual, Jacqueline set out the plates, the long, metal picks and the glasses. She plated the seafood and scooped dollops of mayonnaise onto 2

---

[1] A charming river in Northern France
[2] The factory of Cristal d'Arques

small dishes. Michael, adept at it, opened the oysters with a shucking knife. They sat down and, like they always did on their trips to St Omer, used their fingers instead of knives and forks.

Jacqueline cleared the table and washed the dishes while Michael lay back with a last glass of wine. As it was still raining, and they were both tired, they decided to stay in and to try and sleep, or at least rest, until dinner time.

They still had Saturday and Sunday. Michael needed the time. He wanted their stay to be as perfect as he could make it before he sat Jacqueline down and perhaps, in the park, put his hand on her arm and said, 'Jacqueline, about David…'

It was not in Jacqueline's nature to create an ado and therefore she would not have asked him for explanations. She did not like confrontation. But, since the re-appearance of David, Michael had felt that in the way she looked at him sometimes, in the way she paused on occasions, as if waiting for him to elaborate on what he had said, she was intuitively uneasy in her mind about some annoying intangible incoherence in their lives.

If she would never ask, why then couldn't he keep the charade going? After all, he had lived with his guilt for so many years. They had been happy. In her ignorance, she had been happy. With the advent of David, however, a doubt must have been cast. A doubt which had caused a miniscule shift but which in turn had created mistrust. If he were to guard his secret, surely, twenty, thirty years down the line, on his or her deathbed, he must blurt it out – that their life was a deception, that the concept of their love must be extinguished even as one of their lives was being extinguished. It would be too despicable to guard his guilt beyond the grave.

He felt it was his duty to expose the crystalline crack in that gilded bowl of their lives.[1]

He offered her the last sips of wine from his glass and, taking her in his arms, he lay back with her, and they soon fell asleep.

The rain had stopped and the sun shone through patchily. The deep sleep brought upon him by exhaustion and stress switched seamlessly into wakefulness. Michael opened his eyes, immediately wide awake. He did not wake Jacqueline. By the time he got out of bed and had a shower, Jacqueline would have awakened. He genuinely felt cheerful. They had always been happy at St Omer.

That night they dined at *Le Cygne*. Later, as the evening was fine, they walked to La Place du Maréchal Foch for coffee. The rain earlier on in the day had caused a little chill in the air. He held her close as they walked and, turning slightly to look at her, her cheeks flushed from the wine, he realised that no one else would ever mean as much to him. He stopped and kissed her and her ready response quickened the throbbing in his heart. He was about to say that he

---

[1] Reference to Henry James' 'The Golden Bowl'

loved her but held back. He could not remember the last time he had told her that, but he was certain that she knew.

There was so little that they needed to say to each other. Seeing them together having their coffee, sitting outside *Le Zinc*, a far end bar, passers-by might have made that observation. They might deduce that they were another couple who had been together for too long and who had no common interest and had run out of things to say to each other. They might take heart at their own fresh, conversant relationship and silently vowed never to get into the same, forbidding rut. Looking up at Jacqueline, Michael smiled at how wrong those people would have been. Their little world need not be publicly shared or acknowledged.

He passed the small tablet of chocolate that came with the coffee to her and they continued to sit and watch the world.

David would not have understood that. There was a vivacity in his nature that required expression and sharing and receipt of approbation. His company was always immediately full of fun even to complete strangers. Neither of them could have failed to respond to his affable charm. There was an immediacy in everything he did that came across as genuine and ingenuous.

If David had not turned up again, he would have lived with his guilt, offering Jacqueline everything in his power to make her feel secure and loved and content. But, with David around, Jacqueline was bound to discover some aspects of the truth. It was essential that the facts must come from him.

He was not going to scheme excuses or to position himself with unnecessary explanation in order to win sympathy. He had to be concise and precise and accept her judicial response as stoically as she deserved. He had to be strong for her so that her judgment would not be swayed by sympathy and compassion. She should judge him according to the vile magnitude of his sin.

They would get back to their room. They would make love and rest in each other's arms. There was a storm ahead and he knew she felt it too. They must cling to each other until then. Until then, when needing each other most, they would be wrested apart.

In the morning they had coffee and croissant at the square and strolled through the market. Then they walked along Rue de Dunkerque, Jacqueline to *Sephora* for her Chanel 5 and to purchase little gifts for the people in her office, while he went ahead to the bookshop down the road. Although he could read some French, he loved to have Jacqueline with him when he browsed through the books. But he knew she would come along later.

After an hour walking along the canal, they returned to town for lunch. Jacqueline insisted on having the salade de gésiers[1] at *Le St Charles*, which

---

[1] Gizzard salad

was a small restaurant, intimate and inexpensive. They felt at home there.

The day had dawned bright and sunny, becoming gradually rather oppressive in the afternoon with high humidity and hardly any breeze. Michael suggested that they took the short walk to the park. They decided not to go down to the open formal garden because of the heat and where some children were playing. Instead, they followed the path upwards and at a shady spot between tall beeches, they sat on a wooden bench facing the lake. It was secluded enough at the time of the afternoon for his purpose.

There was an expectant stillness. Time had stood still, waiting to resume. As she sat, instinctively waiting too for Michael to begin, he looked straight into her eyes. He was calm. He knew his moment. It would be a moment of no return. The pattern of their relationship would forever be altered and to no one's advantage. As Tiresias foresaw the horror of the inevitable destiny of Oedipus[1], so Michael foresaw the inevitable annihilation of all his future with her if he were to admit to his sin. To redeem his character, his principles and his self-worth, he knew there was no alternative but to cast the die.

'Jacqueline,' he said, 'about David ...'

---

[1] In Greek Mythology, Tiresias was a blind prophet of Thebes who knew the tragic events in Oedipus' life. Oedipus unknowingly killed his father and married his mother. Tiresias foresaw the tragic events that followed. Oedipus blinded himself and left Thebes. His mother, Jocasta hanged herself.

4 Snowdon – Carl

'It's Jacqueline, isn't it?' she heard a low voice saying behind her as she was about to leave the restaurant. She had come a little late and was told it was full and that she would have to wait.

'I'm Carl. Kay at *Llugwy View* pointed you out to me this afternoon when you arrived. We have rooms on the same floor at the B & B[1],' he explained.

She had had two whiskies in her room before coming out and, through partially closed eyes, she made out this tall man with dark, curly hair and lashes – long dark lashes.

'Hi, pleased to meet you,' she smiled vaguely.

'If you don't mind you could share a table with me. It's really a table for four but it was all that they had left. You could help assuage my guilt of having taken it.'

'Oh, that is kind.'

Michael had long, dark lashes too. That was what registered when he leant slightly to kiss her before

---

[1] Bed and Breakfast

going downstairs and leaving for China. She could not make herself go downstairs with him, not ready yet to forgive and make up, giving him a cold shoulder. From the balcony she saw him disappearing under the apple trees towards the garage. He would be away for 1 to 2 weeks on business and she had decided to get away too. She had to have time to weigh up the situation and see things clearly – to get the emotions out of the way.

What kind of a human being was she, she asked. For so many years, just existing from day to day, perhaps content, perhaps robotic, perhaps too idle to review her life. Michael was her life. But why wasn't she her life? Was what Michael had done wrong or was it heroic and an indication of his devotion to her?

And David, who had been so close a friend, who had held him in such high esteem and with such affection, David was so glibly shunted aside, causing disillusionment in him. She had never suspected such ruthlessness in Michael. What unfathomed abyss had hidden this deviousness? Or was she being hard? Was she unfair? It was after all such a little lie which turned out well for everybody in the end. Should she stand on principles or be a realist?

Carl had said something.

'I said are you staying here long?' he repeated. She drinks, he thought, and then relented and phrased it differently. She had had a few drinks, he reasoned, which did not mean she drank.

'Just for a few days, while my husband is away in China,' she explained.

'What do you intend to do around here, for a few days?'

She re-focused her eyes and, looking closely at him, said, 'there are lots of walks I can enjoy. I'd like to drive around the area again and weather permitting, go up Snowdon.'

He wanted to know if she had climbed Snowdon before, to which she explained that she and Michael had done so several times.

'One of the things he promised me when we got married was that he would take me up Snowdon. We haven't done so for a while now, both of us being so busy. So here I am, all resolute to attempt it by myself.'

They ordered coffee.

'I come once a year to see my mother who lives at Caernarvon. I'm afraid I can only take her in small doses, so I usually stay with Kay and Brian whom I knew from when I was working in Liverpool. Like you, weather permitting, I would climb Snowdon, go on long walks and sit down somewhere quiet and do a few sketches,'

'Is that a hobby, art?'

'I have a little studio cum gallery in London. I paint professionally and I also display works from other artists,' Carl replied.

'I knew many artists long ago when I lived briefly in the south of France. There was more colour and life in some of their lifestyle than in their work. But there were a few really talented ones. Are you a landscape artist?'

Carl hesitated. Here was someone who had lived among artists. Was she going to be one of those judgmental people with little or no talent themselves but who had something to say about everything?

'I do a lot of landscapes and, and some portraits.' In answer to further questions, he explained, 'I make pencil sketches of landscapes, note the light and colour quality and then finish them in oil at the studio or at home. Sometimes a landscape lends itself more to watercolour though, in which case I would accommodate it. Portraits? I prefer oil for those. I am not good enough to capture delicate nuances in watercolour. With oil I can be more forceful, more masculine, and even more ruthless if you like. Everybody starts painting with watercolour but few end their illustrious careers with it. I consider it the most difficult of the mediums.'

Jacqueline was intrigued. She had always admired artistic people as she considered herself miserably without talent.

'Did you always know you could paint or was it something you discovered later?' she asked.

'Oh, much later. I was always quite good at it but it was after university and when I was a teacher. I was friendly with the art teacher and seeing him paint awakened something in me. My first love is still to write though, but with that I really struggle.'

'But you have started on something?' Jacqueline asked.

'Started on too many things. No real sense of direction. You always think this time that's it. You've got the right story line, the right inspiration, and then it frizzles out,' he looked at her with a self-mocking smirk.

'I am, you see, a failure. I am just passable as an artist but not great. My ambition is to write and I can't write.'

'Good Lord, Carl, most of us don't even have a latent passion or talent for anything. You keep trying and you will succeed. Or perhaps you should not try so hard. The right time might come and seize you quite unexpectedly,' she sighed and smiled.

'I think creative people are the luckiest in the world,' she continued.' There is always something alive in you, something striving to be born. Your mind is never still. You are visionaries or potential visionaries. And it does not matter if you never quite gather all these energies together and create something concrete. The creation is a gift to others, but the process of creating is always within your soul, enriching it.'

A surge of inspiration arose within him, so obvious he thought, that he could barely look into her eyes

'When are you going up Snowdon? Why don't we do it together?' he ventured.

Jacqueline looked at him, surprised at his impetuousness, and responded to the latter half of his question.

'I could do with some company, but I am sure I will hold you back. I wouldn't have your energy and stamina.'

'That wouldn't bother me,' he assured her. 'It would be good to slow down a little and enjoy the view,' he said. 'Tomorrow is probably out of the question. I believe it might rain a little, but Tuesday's forecast is good.'

'Tuesday then. I'll go to Beaumaris tomorrow,' she decided.

'And I shall spend a day with my mother,' he laughed heartily, somehow finding the idea amusing.

They had coffee in his room. She sat in the wicker chair by the window. He was pleased at how at ease she was. There was nothing coy about her. Being in a room with a man was not an unfamiliar event and her insouciance relaxed him. There was a lack of fuss in her manner, almost unfeminine, which he found refreshing. She had her coffee black. She did not have to straighten her hair or touch up her face the whole evening. She decided to and sat on the only chair in the room without waiting to be offered. She was like a chum.

With some trepidation he passed one of his very private A5 sketchbooks to her, simply because she saw it on the bed and asked if she might take a look at it. He blushed with embarrassment as she flicked through the pages. He had never allowed anyone else to look at his sketches and wondered why he had not resisted her request.

'They are just sketches. Probably not in your style,' he pre-empted her criticism defensively.

'I have no style. I either like something or dislike it. I am not a critic. I am allowed to be personal,' she answered musingly.

'I knew someone a long time ago who set me right about critics,' she continued, remembering Edward, one winter evening, fuming over a book review in *The Daily Telegraph*.

'You and I, he said, are entitled to our personal opinions however outrageous. But a critic is expressing an opinion to help form the reader's opinion. He has to be fair to both the writer and the reader. He is the interpreter and has no justifiable right to colour or run down a piece of work simply because he personally loves or hates the style or genre. He has to have on his mind a set of forms and rules for a particular genre of writing. He can gauge how closely or errant the writer is from that standard. He can comment on how the writer's adherence or departure from that standard helps, detracts or distracts from his work.'

'It is like parsing a sentence, he used to say,' Jacqueline continued. 'You start with the grammar. If a writer splits his infinitives, bearing in mind that one is judging a piece of creative writing, the critic notes his departure from the correct grammatical form. Then he asks what the intention of the writer is and whether he has achieved his goal and whether it is justifiable at the expense of good grammar. His personal opinions if he expresses them should be as a collateral to the critique and not form the basis of his critique. He should not start by saying that he hates split infinitives and therefore no split infinitive is justifiable. Hopefully, Edward used to say, alluding to Keats, a critic might strive to unweave the rainbow[1] and still be enchanted by its romance.'

Looking directly at him, she concluded, 'So you see, Carl, I am not a critic and my opinions should not count with you. Having said that, I do like the bold strokes and simplicity of your sketches. You should not mind too much what others think. What you think is what gives life and accents and meaning to your work.'

That, it occurred to her, was what made a piece of art or writing so exciting. It excited different sensibilities in different people. Although Michael and she had very similar tastes in books, they differed much in their appreciation of the visual arts.

Some artists and writers might have plenty to say about themselves and their works, but Carl dreaded to think about his own ability, the raison d'être of his art, or how he rated among artists. At the bottom line, he was insecure and unsure of his own talent.

He got out of the bed as Jacqueline rose to leave. They had discussed their trip to Snowdon, agreeing to start very early and that Jacqueline was to prepare some sandwiches. He enquired about her preparation for the climb to which she confirmed that she was ready, having been up Snowdon many times before.

---

[1] Reference to Keats' 'Lamia'.

At the bedroom door, she raised her left hand and placed it on his shoulder, closing in to offer her cheeks to be kissed. He noticed her perfume.

It was Gérard's idea that once a girl had been had, she was a woman. And with womanhood should come sophistication. And there was nothing more unsophisticated than the use of the wrong perfume. He detested the perfume which she sometimes used – a little gift from a school friend. It was girlish. There was no nuance to it.

One day, it was her 18th birthday, he got home early while she was drying her hair in the middle room which ran through to the back room. They used the backroom at Grovelands Road[1] as their bedroom and the middle one as the dressing cum all-purpose storage room. The larger front room was turned into a work place for Gérard, where he had his draughting board, his work desk and a filing cabinet.

That evening he was taking her into London for a meal and then on to a night club.

'Bon anniversaire, ma belle,[2]' he whispered into her ear. He put his arms around her, offering her a small, beautifully wrapped birthday gift. As she fumbled to unwrap it he slipped off her bathrobe and led her into the bedroom.

---

[1] In Reading, Berkshire
[2] Happy birthday, my lovely

Those were the days when the slightest gesture, the slightest tease could send her bubbling with laughter. Laughter, so clear, so unquestioningly uncomplicated, so trusting and infectious came naturally. It was a happy time. And when he made love to her, it was the entirety of her being manifested in a man's love, a man's need. Days and years need not be counted, only the hours till he was home again. He was amusing, popular with people and so knowledgeable for one so young. She was constantly learning from him, adjusting into womanhood with him.

'Mon petit buisson, mon jardin privé, mon jardin parfumé[1],' he dabbed a little Chanel 5 on her lush pubic patch, sending her into giggles. There was often something playfully ridiculous about Gérard's behaviour against his more staid outlook on life.

Du parfum, he said, was a reflection of a woman. It was, to a man, a message. Light, floral scents were for the inexperienced youth. They were playful, fresh and frivolous, but as ephemeral as the spring blossoms that, in their abundance, dazzled and then was gone. They elicited flirtation, but seldom devotion.

A perfume which was too strongly applied was an indiscriminate invitation of a desperate woman, eagerly available, a gaudy draw without the fascination of an enigma.

Always select carefully a perfume of distinction, an expensive perfume which had been carefully created

---

[1] My little bush, my private garden, my perfumed garden

by experts who understood the sensory purpose of each scent. The perfume that she used would become her identity.

She was young, he touched her cheek and added, but so much a woman, someone's mistress, desired. She should use a woman's perfume. As the flowers lend their essence to a perfume, so would a perfume, by a similar process of enfleurage instil its character and its essence onto a woman.

Never sprayed perfume all over. It would be too obvious. She, who already had a man, should place but a little on her left wrist and he would be aware of it. There would be mystery and subtlety, and she should not forget how much more powerful the play on the subconscious was than what was apparent.

So the seasons passed and the years hurried by, but she still clung on to a little Chanel 5 on her left wrist.

Heavy, cloying scent of white gardenias stifled him. Creamy White blossoms everywhere but for a few dark, waxen, green leaves, poking through, here and there. There was a droning of flies and wasps that became louder, approaching. Carl started awake, sitting up in momentary panic. His heart was still beating fast with unease. He had dreamt long dreams. He knew it. But all he could recall were the white gardenias. He had only seen gardenias once, many years ago, on a holiday to Sri Lanka. There was a hedge of gardenia plants along part of the path to the swimming pool. How did that distant insignificant experience manifest itself, out of the blue, out of context this early morning?

Carl opened the window to let in some fresh, cool, cleansing air. He heard the bathroom door shut. There was a common bathroom between the two rooms on the top floor of the B & B. He had suggested that Jacqueline should use it first that morning and to knock on his door when she had finished. He unset the alarm clock on the bedside table and made a cup of strong, black coffee, still feeling vaguely perplexed by the gardenias.

The previous evening he had gone with his mother and his step-father to a pub after an early tea. He did not stay long, giving the early start for the climb up Snowdon as an excuse. He could have stayed for much longer but he was anxious to get back to Betws-y-Coed. It filled him with guilt for he had much love for his mother. She had brought him up single-handedly and they had been very close when he was a child. He owed her, but they had grown apart over the years as life took them in different directions. She had married when he was 18 and he had gone to university and then, after a short spell in the area, had moved to London. One day he must ask her up to London and spend some quality time with her. He must.

The thought of his mother often cast a gloom over him. She had a hard time bringing him up on her own and he would have wanted her to go out into the world, travel, live, discover herself and become a more rounded person. Instead she had lived all her life in

177

Blackpool, got married, moved to Caernarvon and remained there. It was a reflection of what his own life had been and might become again, and that depressed him. It was so easy to settle into a life, into a relationship, into a pattern of activity or inactivity, into a corner rather than living it.

He knew that asking Jacqueline to climb Snowdon with him after just one meeting was perhaps a little rash on his part because he was not usually impulsive with people. Unlike the women he usually met and befriended, Jacqueline interested him immediately with her conversation and her insights.

When you are in your forties, have been married, had two kids and divorced, you would begin to feel insecure, to take stock and to either act like a pathfinder, sensing out what you consider the appropriate path, or simply to be accepting and fall in with what comes your way. Carl was more inclined towards the latter gestalt. Rather than striding forward, an architect of his own life, he was willing to allow the pattern of his life to emerge from the interpolation of events that happened his way.[1]

They arrived at Pen-y-Pas early, just after 6am, in order to ensure a parking space. The air was cold and there was a lingering trace of water-coloured mist in the valleys. The sun, silhouetting the distant hills behind them as they trod along, already promised a fine day. Carl did not take going up Snowdon as a

---

[1] Reference to the Theory of Gestalt

sport. It was just good, healthy exercise, an opportunity to get away from London and to clear his mind. Unlike most people who went up as a group or as a couple, he had always preferred his own company. On this occasion, he accommodated the slower pace of Jacqueline, but he was glad that she appeared to be occupied with her own thoughts and he was not required to fabricate any conversation.

It surprised him a little at how prepared Jacqueline was for the climb. She had the proper climbing boots, which protected the ankles. He could see that she had layers of clothes on which she could easily remove if it got too warm. Her backpack was light and just big enough to contain her rain proof jacket and trousers if the weather turned bad. She had her bottle of water and the sandwiches she had agreed to prepare. There was no frill about her. A soft, grey woollen cap framed her face which was free from any make-up.

When they reached the causeway at *Llyn Llydaw*[1], they turned around as the sun broke over the hills behind them, turning the water of the lake, on that still morning, into a mirrored glare.

They laughed into the sun at this sudden change. For the first time that morning, Carl felt an affinity with her and was able to look closely at her. It surprised him even more at how stark and exposed that face stood

---

[1] A natural lake on the way up Snowdon on the Miner's Track – separated into 2 parts by the man-made causeway

out in the sun, with her hair pushed back and the face framed, like an exhibit, by the grey cap.

He could not discern her age, but she was certainly older than he was and certainly older than the impression he had of her, having seen her mainly in the night. There were soft crow's feet beside her eyes as she laughed and lines on her brow. He noticed that she never abandoned herself to a full, relaxed smile or laughter. There was a tautness to her jaws that showed a certain amount of control, as if she was afraid to let go. It occurred to him that she was not beautiful, but almost immediately retracted that opinion as being unfair. He was judging her against his ex-wife, Becchi.

Standing there then in the full sunshine, Becci would have been stunning. Even in the stillness of that morning, her long, wavy, blonde hair would have appeared to be flowing. Her arched eye-brows, her large transparent blue eyes, her full lips – always in the brightest of red lipstick, her figure and her bosom, would turn any man's head and captivate his heart as they had captivated his. Her look of innocence and wide-eyed vulnerability could stand up to scrutiny under whatever light. Women like her exuded their sexuality and their femininity in a primeval appeal to the males of the species.

Jacqueline's look was harsher, interestingly weathered with a hidden narrative of a past. Becchi's impact was immediate, complete, full-on. She was a display of the finest jewellery under spotlights. With Jacqueline one required time and a spirit of adventure to discover what might be hidden in the deepest mines. From an artist's perspective, Jacqueline would make a more creative subject.

At *Llyn Glaslyn*, the Blue Lake, the sun's glare was replaced by the clearest reflections of the surrounding hills and the wispy cirrus clouds in the soft blue morning sky. As there was no hurry to get to the summit, Carl and Jaqueline rested on a boulder by the lake to admire the view. Both of them knew how often the views up to Snowdon were shrouded in gloomy fogs or spoilt by ceaseless rain.

'You live in London, but I detect a slight northern accent,' Jacqueline commented.

'I am born and bred in Blackpool,' he replied. 'My mum always said I am a real Sandgrown'un.'

'A sand what?'

'A Sandgrown'un,' he laughed. 'That's a person who is born in Blackpool. I was actually conceived on the sands of Blackpool according to my mother and that makes me a thoroughbred Sandgrown'un. You are the genuine stuff, Carl, she used to say – you will endure.'

'I have never come across that expression, but how fascinating. It must have been a most romantic conception for your mother to be so specific and to dwell on it.'

Carl looked quizzically at her. He certainly had never looked at it from that angle. 'I suppose you could interpret it as that if you do not know the circumstances,' he said. 'The consequences, I can assure you, belied that.'

'But the consequence was YOU,' Jacqueline said, 'and that is not a bad thing.'

'My mother never quite got over it.'

'Ah, I see,' Jacqueline added, 'it did not end well.'

'It ended as it had started – suddenly. Like a storm that blew in and blew out again. I never knew my father. All I know is that he had just graduated from medical school and was down at Blackpool on holidays – staying with some friends. My mother was working at a guest house and somehow they met and within 3 days he had gone away. He was a very good looking bloke according to mum and very well spoken. All mum knew was his name and that his family came originally from Shropshire but had moved by that time to Glasgow. She did not think he should be burdened with a baby when he was just setting up in life, and in those days there would have been no way of finding him.'

Helping her to sling her backpack on, he led on towards the Screes. There was no one distinct way to scramble up the huge randomly strewn boulders but they only had to decide which group of climbers, who had passed them at Llyn Glaslyn, to follow. Fortunately, the fine weather made the climb easy and Carl was relieved that although she was often on all fours, Jacqueline had managed to manoeuvre her way up without his help. On a few occasions he thought it would be the manly thing to do to hold on to her and give her a push up, but somehow he felt a little bashful and awkward.

They had passed the point where the Pyg Track joined the Miner's and the path had become an uneven paved rock surface. Still rising, it then began to zig-zag towards the crest of the ridge which then led on the left to the summit and to Crib Goch on the right. Jacqueline stopped and rested on the low rock wall, commenting on the looming mist that had appeared from the far side of the ridge and begun to roll and merge down towards them.

'Have you tried contacting your father?' she asked, as they settled down to the sandwiches she had brought.

He thought for a moment and then replied, 'I had toyed with the idea many a time, but never garnered enough courage to pursue it further. One gets so caught up with day to day events to really assign time for the purely speculative. I suppose I am afraid of finding out about him and how he would react to discovering he has a grown up son all along. Has he a family of his own? What are they like? Would we be socially compatible? There are so many questions. What if they would not accept me? Worse still, what if I could not accept them?' he paused.

'There are always questions in life and the answers are not always palatable. You need to balance what you are and what you have against what you might become if you do trace him. My parents have been dead a good many years and I hardly think about them now. Would it have affected me if I had not known them? I suppose I would have been curious. My father and I had been estranged for many years before he died and mother, much as I cared for her, was not a potent force in my life. For me life started when I had left home. You see, Carl, people, they often disappoint in the end.'

He looked round at her. He took what she said as a confidence. He was surprised at such cynicism. Such bitterness stated so peremptorily as a fact.

'Would your mother mind if you were to make contact?' she asked.

'Mother is not keen on it at all. To my mother it was an insignificant event and would have been long forgotten if it wasn't for me being born.'

'I have been prattling on,' he laughed. 'I know nothing about you – but I feel we are friends.'

'We'll see, we'll see,' she replied. She stood up, put things back into her backpack and then continued up towards the peak. Carl realised that he had talked more about him than he had ever done to anyone else. Somehow it had not felt like an exposure because Jacqueline was a stranger and there was no existing or potential relationship to be compromised.

With the fog rolling in fast and dense, they only stopped to refresh themselves, had a coffee and then turned back down towards the Pyg Track. Although without the tricky footwork required of the Screes on the way up, the Pyg Track was a more rocky route for most of the way. They made their way down mostly in silence. Carl wanted to ask about her. He wanted to know what she was doing on her own at Snowdonia. He knew, from what she had mentioned before and from a phone call she had received earlier in the day, that she had a husband. He wanted to de-mystify the cynicism that always lurked behind her comments.

They laughed about a couple of women who were carrying umbrellas and handbags on their climb as if they were out on an after-dinner stroll. Taking the opportunity, he commented that it was the first time he had seen her laugh in so relaxed a manner. She appeared to be surprised.

'I wasn't aware of being such an open book. I have things on my mind. Have I been such bad company?' she asked.

'Not at all. Just a little intriguing. You want to unload some of it on me? After going on about myself since we met, it would be a happy change for me to learn a little about you.'

'And where would that lead? Tell you what, depending on how I feel later, it might be the exact therapy I need. We'll see how it goes.' She left it at that.

The room appeared dark against the square of curtained light at the window. After a quick shower when they got back from Snowdon, he had closed the curtains from the harsh afternoon light before sinking into the bed and falling quickly into a dreamless sleep. They had agreed to meet for dinner if nothing more pre-occupying cropped up. His watch showed a quarter to 7 but the now overcast sky had made it seem much later. Peering out of the window, he noticed that it must have rained earlier on. The back garden was wet and a slight mist had risen and hovered among the trees.

A short note had been left through the bottom of the door. She had gone to Betws-y-Coed and would see him at the *Hen Siop*[1], the local fish and chip shop, at about 7.30. He gave his face a quick splash, wetted his hair, combed through it and then ruffled it up. It should not take more than 10 minutes to get to the *Hen Siop* and he hurried there.

Looking inside but not seeing her there, he carried on deeper into town. At the bridge over the River Llugwy, he stopped and saw her sitting among the large boulders in the river where, after the heavy rain of the previous weeks, the water roared down as a waterfall. She was lost in thoughts but, after a short while, as if she could sense his presence, she turned around and looked up. He found her sudden smile as refreshing as the cascading water.

He doubted if he could have been intrigued by her if she had been constantly and vacuously happy. He liked a woman to be cryptic, to present him with clues to grapple with. An inscrutable face that suddenly almost revealed, but not quite, appealed to his curiosity. He wanted to know about her. He wanted to know her. He walked towards the other end of the

---

[1] Welsh for Old Shop

bridge as she came up and greeted her gently on the cheeks.

'Are you still game for the fish and chips?' he asked.

'You know, I am famished and I can't think of anything better or faster,' she replied. 'You had a sound sleep I guess. I didn't want to wake you. See what I have bought for the girls at work.' She showed him a few fridge magnets in the shape of sheep with dangling legs on cords, and continued, 'Nothing imaginative, but I know they would love them.'

'Aren't you tired after the climb?' he enquired.

'Not after I've had a shower, no. But I feel wearied. Come, let's go and eat. Who knows, I might even bare my soul and cast my heavy spirits upon your shoulders later,' she said mockingly.

Picking up the tenor of self-mockery he replied, 'I'm a Sandgrown'un, you know. My shoulders are broad.'

There was a fine, cold drizzle when they left the *Hen Siop*. He put an arm around her as they ran across the road to the grey stone *Pont-y-Pair Inn* and managed to get a corner table in the warm and busy bar. The recognition of camaraderie made them laugh like old friends. In a lightning flash, Jacqueline also recognised how much she had missed Michael. The countless times they had laughed together without having to say a word. It also recalled their early days at Watford, on their own or with David.

Carl could see the transition of her carefree laughter into a sad, poignant smile. He felt they were treading on shadows, tracing some faint imprints of her past. He would not have it. Instead of his usual pint, he matched her whisky to whisky, hers neat, his on the rock. The present must be the master of the past.

'You said you are divorced, do you have someone in your life?' she asked, for something to say.

'Now and then – here and there,' he replied. 'Nothing serious and nothing permanent.'

'Having been married for some time, don't you miss the companionship?'

'Don't get me wrong, Becchi is a very kind and good person, but we never had that depth in our relationship, that something which is distinctly her, that I missed. I suppose one woman has been very much the same as the other to me at the moment. That is probably my fault for not allowing the time and the generosity to know them better. Sad to say, Jacqueline, they just haven't interested me enough.'

'Play the field if you like as long as you don't lead them on. Women today are as capable of playing the mating game as you men. It is the lies which we find incomprehensible and unacceptable.' she asserted.

'I assure you we feel the same. The problem arises when one party takes casually what the other offers with intensity. You are not playing the same game then,' he said.

'What people these days called *not being on the same page*?' she asked and began to laugh.

'Come,' she stood up and took her handbag which was hanging from the back of her chair. 'Shall we go?' she suggested. 'And if your shoulders are still broad enough, Carl,' she hesitated and then added, '- we'll see.'

Through the rising mist the finest drizzle continued to fall onto the already wet and slippery road. Jacqueline clicked open her small umbrella and handed it to Carl to carry. They hurried along through the dismal night to *Llugwy View*.

He could feel her shivering as she fumbled for the front door key. He quickly took out his from his jacket pocket and opened the door. All he wanted at the moment was to protect her. The anomaly between the certainty and strength of her observations when she spoke and this sudden physical frailty unsettled him. There was a moment of disorientation.

'Are you alright?' he asked. 'Would you like to come over for a coffee?'

'Let me have a shower and I'll see you later.'

The heating was on in the room. He re-set it to a lower temperature and opened his window a little. The mist had thickened quickly and he could hardly see the end of the back garden. He plumped up the cushion on the wicker chair and tidied his bed. Not knowing how long Jacqueline would take, he did not make the coffee, but put some water to boil. He could quickly re-heat it when she came.

When he heard her coming, he got out of bed to shut the window and put the kettle to boil again. She knocked softly on the door. Her hair had been washed and blow-dried and she wore a white, loose and light V-neck cotton top with a little embroidery in white along the V over a mid-blue sarong. The faint perfume that emanated from her created an ambience of inchoate intimacy. He offered her a cup of black coffee and as she chose to sit on the wicker chair, he sat on his bed against the head-board.

'Carl,' she began, 'thank you so much for keeping me company the last 2 days. It has prevented me from wallowing in introversion. But I had a lot of thinking to do and it was pleasanter doing it in your company than on my own.' She sipped her coffee, stood up, walked to the window, opened half the curtain and looked out into the gloom cast night.

'How murky,' she remarked and turning round to face Carl she continued, 'why, that's the exact state of my mind. I am trying to find somewhere to start in order to put things into perspective, to have a sense of what is important and what is not. So please excuse me if I meander a little.'

'At the time when I first met Michael, my life was in limbo. A few years before, a long term relationship had ended. I was just 16 when I met Gérard and it decided the course of my life. When you are so young and dreamy and a good looking Frenchman takes a second look at you and pursues you, how could you not feel flattered? So I got straight into a relationship with him that lasted many years.

When he left me to go back to France and to his wife, I just existed from day to day. I had had no experience of life outside of being with him and I could not envisage any kind of future besides staying put in

Reading. A few years later, I went to meet up with him at Düsseldorf and he did not turn up. I told myself – what the heck. I might as well take life by the horns, be in control and live it up. And I gave it a good ride.

You see, Carl, I spent almost 3 years living in Germany and France and met and lived with some interesting people. I don't think I was even trying to get to know myself. I was trying to get to know people, to gauge them and to discover a safe centre of gravity from where I would not get hurt again.

When I finally met up with Gérard in France, I realized what a waste of time and of my life it had all been. I decided to put away the past and to start again. By that time my mother had died and I was left a lot of money. I thought, I had hardly any education at all. So I applied to go to Watford and did a course in advertising. And there I met Michael,' she paused and asked if she could have another cup of coffee. Without a word she left the room and came back with a small bottle of whisky.

'I thought then that I was stronger and wiser and more adroit at handling men. But Michael, you see, was so different from anyone I had ever met. There was this serious demeanour in one so young. I enjoyed the way he talked, the way he hesitated before saying something and his laughter when he considered something as funny. But most of all, Carl, I admired his integrity. He was a person of principles. I trusted him more than anyone else I knew.

There were the three of us – Michael, David and I. Michael and David were the best of friends – really hardly separable. They had a year together before I came into the scene. It was Michael who first became my friend, but there were times when I felt I was the third party. I think at some time or other we must all have felt that way.'

She moved dreamily towards the bed and sat on the edge facing Carl. She topped up his small glass of whisky and continued.

'David was just the opposite of Michael. He was a happy person. He appeared carefree and was always ready with a practical joke. I had never known him to be stressed – he always seemed many degrees below the stress level. He was perhaps what I needed at the time. Michael and I were the best of friends and I could talk with him more freely and intelligently than to anyone else, but we were stuck in that dimension. If he had taken it further he would have expected commitment and I was not ready for that. But he did not really make his move and David did,' she smiled guiltily and got up and walked up and down the room. Then she opened the window slightly and, leaning back against it, continued.

'It was a happy time. I have such fond memories of our days at Watford. In the summer of 77 Michael and I happened across David with a girl while we were out walking in the park. I saw red. I felt insulted. It was demeaning. We were such great friends, the three of us. I could even understand his cheating on someone because he did not take life too seriously, but that he should have cheated on me, a close friend, I found unforgiveable. I refused to see him or listen to his explanations – excuses – as I thought they would be. Through that last term, Michael was there for me and there for David. My respect and feelings for him grew immensely then.' She paused, as if to ponder the situation.

Feeling rather cramped sitting against the head of the bed, Carl got up and asked if she would like some coffee. He was engrossed in what she had told him, and was eager to find out where it would lead. He found the intimacy of Jacqueline baring her soul to him, veil by veil, softly, undramatically, more erotic than if she had stood naked before him. He moved back and sat on the edge of the bed, waiting unobtrusively for her to continue.

'We never saw David again after college until I walked into my office one day in August and there he was. He had been using my company to help him with recruitment the past few months and I never knew of it. I was genuinely happy to see him and I thought – here was a chance to make up to Michael for losing his dear friend.'

Carl could see a rising restlessness and nervous energy in her as she paced the room. She had crossed her arms across her bosom, her taut hands, moving slightly a she spoke.

'From something he said, Carl, I discovered that my take on what happened at Watford, when I saw him with the girl, was wrong. She was Gloria, his girlfriend of some months, and he was breaking up with her. And Michael knew it all along.'

'All the charade he played, all the innuendos, all his support for me and David were founded on deception. I know how hard it must have been for him to play this unnatural role – how much he must have loved me or be infatuated with me – to sink to that level. He must have suffered over the years living with this lie. I know him well enough to know that. But I find it so hard to forgive him, and not to be deeply disappointed with him.' she sighed and shook her head.

'Why is it that we could forgive and excuse people who are weak and wicked so much more easily than people we love and respect? And I miss him so Carl,' she cried. 'It's like losing a twin, a part of my consciousness.'

'I miss being close to him, feeling his touch, his breath on my neck and on my shoulders. You know, it was almost two years from when we met that Michael first made love to me? I didn't know what to expect and I thought it wasn't important. But it was. It was. I discovered that when somebody makes love to you because he wanted you, it usually falls far short of when somebody makes love to you because he loved you. And he loved me, Carl.'

Carl asked if she would mind if he opened the window a little wider. He got up and stood with her by the window as she poured the last drop of whisky into her glass and offered it to him. He took a small sip and returned it to her. She certainly needed it more than he did, he thought.

'With Michael, I realized that being loved was not just a passive thing – not just an acceptance of what was offered. It was a live wire. It sizzled into your bones and kept your heart and mind positive to whatever the world has to throw at you. Oh Carl, when I picture him now, I could burst, I could burst.'

She flung her arms to her side in exasperation and looking straight at him and in a soft raspy voice dared him. 'Fuck me Carl, fuck me before I go crazy.'

Taking her in his arms, Carl kissed her, wondering how someone could love another so perilously. He refused to dwell on how he would be compared to Michael.

Morning brought awkwardness, a little embarrassment and a confused resentment that he had been used. Her car was no longer on the road when he went down to breakfast. Kay mentioned, to his relief, that she had gone out early towards Portmeirion. He had promised to visit his mother and have lunch with her. In the past two days he had thought more about her. It might be an opportunity to find out more about his father, although she had always been rather reticent about the whole affair.

Afterwards, he would take his sketch book with him and try to go a little way up the less frequented Rhyd

Ddu path until he had a good view of *Cwm[1] Clogwyn* on Llechog Ridge, if the fog had lifted by then. He remembered how spectacular it was the last time he saw it. He needed to be alone, somewhere quiet, to relax into his usual self.

Dorothy Reyes, Dot to her family and friends, savoured the last drag of her cigarette before stubbing it out on an ashtray. She tossed the stale butts into the kitchen bin and ran the ashtray under the tap. Then she opened the large window of her sitting room and picking up the ever-ready can of air freshener from behind the TV screen, squirted a few sprays into the room. Joe, her husband, had already left to play darts with a few friends, and she was expecting her son Carl to arrive very soon. Knowing how Carl hated the smell of cigarettes and the very idea of them, she usually tried to clear the air as much as she could. Carl, as she knew so well, was likely to give her a lecture on her smoking.

She was proud of her son. And of herself. For the first eighteen years of his life she had struggled to give him a reasonable life and seeing him through University later on. She was proud that he was the first person in her family to go to University. She knew he was of good stock. From his father's side, he had inherited intelligence and probably his artistic bent.

---

[1] A steep sided hollow on a mountainside or at the head of a valley usually caused by glacial erosion

From her side, she would like to believe, he had acquired determination and real grit. Her people were unsophisticated but tough as nail, real survivors.

Occasionally, she could glimpse something of his father's smile in him, but she was aware that the passage of time must play tricks on the memory. After all, she was with Adrian for only – was it 3 days? Perhaps just a few days more – and it was well over forty years ago. She would like to believe that Adrian would have been pleased with how Carl had turned out to be if he had known him.

It saddened her when Carl and Becchi divorced for she was very fond of Becchi. She hardly ever saw the grandchildren who now lived in The Netherlands. Every night she prayed for Carl's happiness. These artistic people, she told herself often, were dreamers. She was practical. She had to be. Sometimes she felt that Carl was disappointed in her. He would have her more ambitious, more knowledgeable, better read and perhaps less common. But all she ever needed was to have a house and home, security, a little love and Carl's happiness. More than Joe, more than herself, he was the meaning of her existence and the source of her worries. After all, what would her life have been if he had not come along? She quickly stemmed that thought.

When Carl got married, Dot thought her duty was done. He could not have picked a lovelier person than Becchi. If Dot had a daughter, she would have wanted her to be just like Becchi. They got on really well because Becchi had such a gentle and warm nature. When the girls arrived in the first three years of their marriage, everything appeared so complete. But Carl's drifting nature, Dot thought with some bitterness, destroyed all that. The marriage lasted just over six years.

It was to Becchi's credit that she had maintained a relationship with Dot and with Carl. Once or twice a year, Carl would visit the children and sometimes they would come over to London. When he was in Leiden, he would often stay with Becchi and her husband Hugo. They lived in a large farm house with a guest wing. Becchi made sure that Dot saw her granddaughters when they visited England and had invited her to stay with them at Leiden. It was important to Dot that her grandchildren knew Carl's side of the family. She often wondered how Carl could have allowed his marriage to break up when he himself understood what it was like to grow up without a father.

When Carl was very young, Dot had to leave him with her parents for a large part of the day in order to work at a guest house. In spite of that they were very close. However, she felt that her parents indulged him too much. Being an only child, he never really learned how to share or to see things from another person's point of view. Although always a good looking and friendly lad and always very popular at school, he was also self-centred. Dot blamed herself for not being a better mother.

She knew that Carl was a sociable person and was in and out of relationships. What worried her was the aloneness he would feel when he had grown older. The girls were already in their mid-teens and when they had gone out into the world and started their own life, an absent father would be located at the periphery.

The girls kept in touch with her on the telephone and sent her photos by email. They exchanged birthday and Christmas cards and gifts. They allowed her the role of a grandmother. This, Dot accepted, was more than they had allowed Carl the role of a father. They had grown up with Hugo, who was a wonderful parent to them. This, Dot conceded, was as it should be, but in the depth of her mind, she wished Carl could have played a greater role in their lives.

Dot would like Carl to be steadier and find someone permanent in his life. She believed that a woman could cope with loneliness better than a man. She had at her resources more freedom of expression – she could cry, she could confide, she could be more stoical than a man.

Carl roughed up his hair which his mother had just smoothed down as he greeted and kissed her. He had been thinking more about his mother lately and sincerely wished he could treat her more kindly and show more appreciation of what she had done for him. However, he ruffled up his hair just as reflexively as his mother had to smooth it. He had a cup of coffee in the morning with Kay and Brian and skipped breakfast in order to get to Caernarvon early. They were going to the *Tafarn Y Porth*[1]. He had learned over the years not to suggest any other restaurant. It was her local and she could get the sort of food she was familiar and happy with.

He ordered a traditional breakfast with a mug of tea and a large glass of red wine for his mother and a breakfast sandwich and half an IPA[2] for him. He could not build up an appetite and was rather fractious. The prickly experience of the previous night clung to him like a tenacious burr. He was anxious to do his duty by his mother and then get away to Snowdon.

'Why aren't you having a proper meal? This is not going to last you long,' Dot exclaimed

'I am not that hungry. I had a large meal last night,' Carl explained.

'Even so. You must take care of yourself. As I keep saying, you must settle down. Wait too long and it might be too late.'

'I'm alright.'

Carl disliked intensely to talk about himself and especially to be the topic of conversation. He had wanted to ask Dot about Adrian, but as he had so tersely refused to talk about himself, he did not feel justified in questioning her about his father. Besides, she would probably come out with the same argument that she knew very little of his background and that it would not be fair to disrupt his life with the discovery

---

[1] The Gate Inn – name of a pub now a Wetherspoon Pub
[2] Indian Pale Ale

that he had a grown son. It was just a brief holiday affair and he should not be made to face up to its consequence. She would then ask him how he would react if one of his many girlfriends turned up with a child in tow. What if he had not even liked the woman?

'Would you like to come up to London and stay a week with me in December? We can then go over to see the girls at Leiden just before Christmas.'

'That would be very nice. Have you asked Becchi about it?'

'She mentioned it the last time I spoke to her. We could stay over a weekend perhaps,' Carl suggested.

He was glad that another decision was made and was eager to get to Snowdon. A gentleness descended on him when he took his leave of her – a feeling of gratitude and affection and a need to acknowledge them. He gave her a generous hug and kissed her on the forehead.

A light and steady breeze from the Irish Sea blew over the Menai Strait[1], fetching with it a thick, metamorphous fog that banked against *Cwm Clogwyn*, rising silently to its rim. The peachy glow where the sun from a patchy sky struck it, foiled against the softer whites and greys where it was shaded, gave it an eerie depth of gently changing forms.

Carl did a quick sketch of it, noting the variation of tones. He wanted to capture the fullness of the fog and

---

[1] A narrow stretch of shallow tidal water between the island of Anglesey and mainland Wales

suggest the plasticity in their shapes. Because he could not see the precipitous drop of the cwm or the view of distant lakes and valleys, it was imperative that he should evoke a dimension of depth. He pencilled in the jagged edge of the cwm where the fog had only just begun to invade. He wanted to show the contrast between the vaporous, mysterious and invasive fog and the sharpness and permanence of the static edge. He outlined the fluid areas of moss mingled with short grass and the exposed, smooth, lichen covered rocks.

The fast encroaching fog prevented him from moving further towards the peak. He retraced his steps resignedly. The rain of the previous week had made the ground rather soggy, but the carpet of short grass and mosses prevented the walk from becoming a muddy one. Half way down he stopped and sat on the low stone wall of the ruin of an old mining shelter. He wanted to share the views with Jacqueline. He wanted to rush back and describe the cwm to her and explain the colours and sounds of this wilderness to her. Snowdon and Snowdonia as a whole had always been inspirational to him as an artist. But the difference, he sensed that day, was that he felt aspirational. He wanted to achieve. He wanted to create. He wanted to paint. He also wanted to write. All his senses were quickened in a liveliness of frustration in need of expression.

Looking down in front of him, he began to sketch what he saw – the short quivering grass, the damp mosses and the sparkle of water that trilled in little runnels downhill. He took in the countless flat, broken pieces of grey and worn slate from an old mine and the colours of the lichens on the walls and rocks – dappling of grey, brown, orange, green and vibrant yellow.

Picking up a small piece of slate, he stared blankly at it for a moment and then on its smooth, dark grey surface, he carved carefully with his Swiss Army knife – '*If Chance will have Me King…*'[1]

The shower cubicle steamed. He had turned the hot water on to a high setting. As in a ritual he cleaned himself from head to toes, taking his time, rubbing deep into his scalp, into every part of his body that he could reach. He felt cleansed of his past – not of his past life, but of the person that he used to be. He felt sloughed of the great, insidious disease of apathy. He would build on his limited experience of life. He would be more focussed on people, on events and on his surroundings. He had to reach out in order to trawl in the richness of life and he had the renewed stir to write again. A spurt of new confidence had sprung out of his encounter with Jacqueline. This was his renaissance.

As for what had happened the previous night, he dismissed it as just another parcel of memory. He felt that he understood Jacqueline. She had needed an outlet, so wound up was she with self-doubt and self-searching. He was her therapy. She was the seed to his

---

[1] Reference to Macbeth: If chance will have me king, why, chance may crown me, without my stir

imagination. It was not an unpleasant coupling of interests.

He dried himself vigorously, feeling flushed, alive, and full of expectation. He opened his room window wide, letting the cool evening air tingle his body, reviving him like rain on a wilting plant. He pulled on a T-shirt and a jumper over it and, in case it rained, he slung on his jacket and ran briskly downstairs and out into the street.

He wanted to look for Jacqueline in town. But it was no longer about her. It was about him. She was the fount of energy from which he would re-charge. He was not worried about her. She was strong and would always come through. He hoped he had helped her to de-stress and to relax. But he, he was on a high, on the sharp edge of sensation.

In the fading light, she sat on a bench in the garden opposite the shops where she had bought a postcard, writing a few lines to Clinger. She had thought about her the last few days, of her children, her farm, and her husband. How would Clinger have dealt with the situation with Michael, she wondered. Clinger, she told herself, would have done the right wifely thing and had forgiven him. Clinger, with her nature so embracing and protective, would have enfolded him and said, now, now, she understood. Jacqueline almost envied Michael this. She too would have liked a Clinger in her life to hold on to her and to say, hush, hush now, she understood. Clinger and she genuinely liked each other, but Jacqueline knew that Clinger would never have understood her. She stuck the stamps on the card and went looking for a post box.

Carl had seen her on the bench but, as she was absorbed in writing, had refrained from joining her. He walked a little way out of town and turned around to find her posting the card. He walked up to her and said 'Hello'.

'Oh Carl, you gave me a fright. I was miles away,' she laughed.

'Away back home?'

'Oh no, I was away in Tasmania. I have just posted a card to a dear friend who lives there. I was just remembering when Michael and I spent some time with her a few years ago.'

'How about dinner? I am famished,' Carl suggested.

'My favourite pastime. Let's go.'

They had so much to tell each other of what they had done during the day. Jacqueline had been to Beddgelert, where she had not been for many years, and noticed anew the character and the colours of the stone walls of the cottages. She had stood a long time on the bridge watching a few seemingly stationary fish, with the slightest flick of the tail-fins, braving the swift flow of the clear shallow stream. With the help of local signs, she then followed a circular nature trail.

Carl spoke of his walk up Rhyd Ddu path and the sketches he had made. Jacqueline expressed an interest in looking at them later in the evening. Both were relieved at how freely they could talk without being embarrassed by what had happened the previous evening. Jacqueline accepted it as one of those things which could happen without further significance or consequence and she thought Carl had handled it with unexpected maturity. She enjoyed his company and affirmed in her mind that his acquaintance was worth the while.

Guided by the lights from buildings and the pubs they made their way in the unexpected fog towards *Llugwy View*. Outside the *Pont-y-Pair Inn* Carl remembered the piece of slate he had carved.

'Here's something I picked up on Snowdon this afternoon,' he stopped and presented it to her.

'Oh, thanks. I do like unexpected gifts,' she smiled, rubbed it in her hand and read the inscription.

'*If chance will have me king...*' she read it aloud. She had goose bumps all over her arms. Looking at him in a quizzical manner, she added, 'Beware what you wished for Carl. Remember, *uneasy lies the head that wears a crown.*'[1]

As if she could not let it rest, as they walked on, she said, 'You see, Carl, Macbeth did make a stir. He committed murders and never had full faith in the witches' prophesies. It is always dangerous to dwell on the equivocation of forces beyond our understanding.'

Putting the piece of slate in her handbag, she turned around to him and said, 'I love it.'

There are so many ways at looking at things, Carl thought. He was too apt to accept things at face value.

---

[1] William Shakespeare Henry IV, Part Two.

He was too lazy and too afraid to analyse. His ability to connect ideas was on a single plane. Oh God, he thought, there is a whole world of exploration opened to him. He looked at Jacqueline and turning her around he said, 'Thank you Jacqueline, thank you so much.'

'What have I done to deserve this, Carl? I thought I was the one to be thankful. You had kept me company and listened so patiently to me,' she said in surprise.

'Oh no, Jacqueline. If I had done anything at all it had been with pleasure. I feel like a cocktail of chemicals, shaken up and jostling within me, full of potential but destined to remain inert, until a single catalyst comes accidentally along and sets it alive, afire. It is most odd. I feel potent and propelled towards some undiscovered spaces.'

'And when you finally come down to earth, Carl, don't come down too fast or too low. Attain a fair balance, but keep that distant goal in view.'

This feeling, welling in him, a want to express, a want to share, but he did not know how. He wanted to appear calm and mature, but he did not know how.

He was a miniscule speck in space, within a universe of distant stars, of galaxies and nebulae and, in awe, he did not know on what to focus. How far, how very far more, had he to go in order to develop the facility of self-control, to garner the diverse germs of the imagination within the fold of ideas and narrative, and to be able to communicate? So wound and twisted was this core desire that when it ever became unsprung, he would need all the discipline in the world to control its flow. He needed guidance.

By the time Jacqueline came back to his room, he had the coffee ready. She had gone to dry the dampness from the fog on her hair. Her face was flushed and aglow from the day spent outdoors. She had changed into comfortable, loose, unbleached cotton trousers and a loose top in a darker shade of beige. She sat on the edge of the bed and asked to see the sketches Carl had made during the day. He sat beside her and explained that he had only done two sketches that day but there were a few others from before he met her.

There were pretty views of mountains with scree, of narrow courses of water lacing down the slopes, and of lakes and their attendant rocks. But the last two sketches had a vitality of their own. The artist was not viewing from a distance but was confronting what he saw. The strokes were bolder, had more conviction and were fewer. A few brush-overs with the thumb or a finger had given depth and fullness to the advancing fog and a few stout strokes brought out the contrasting jaggedness of some rocks.

'I would love to see these when they are completed, Carl. I think they are so alive, so reflective of a state of mind.'

'I'll invite you over to see them when they are ready,' Carl offered.

There was a moment of awkward silence. Carl got up to put away his sketch book and Jacqueline got up and walked towards the window. Turning around, she asked if Carl would like to join her for lunch the next day.

'I don't have to rush back. Michael won't be back till the day after. I thought we could get some fish and chips and have them by the river.'

Although he knew that she would be leaving the following day, Carl had stashed the thought away in a recess of his mind. It was as if as long as the fact had not been pronounced, there was no finality to it. She had told him earlier that Michael had cut short his visit to China.

'Sure, I would love that. I would miss having you around,' he admitted.

'I'm afraid I have not been the figure of fun that you might wish to have with you on a holiday. Those days are long gone. When one is young one wants to please and impress and thinks that one's job is to be fun and entertaining – as if that is the only means of acquiring affection and admiration. These days I am rather staid.'

'I think you are fun. Not in a heady, inane way. I find you inspirational.'

'Look at me Carl. No, I mean really look at me. What is there inspirational in me? Nothing! It is the aspiration within you that has caused the inspiration. I am but a reflective index. Perhaps we are well met after all,' she said with a faint, unselfconscious twinkle in the eyes.

'See you tomorrow then,' he replied.

'Tomorrow.'

The next day dawned indifferently. There was a remnant of fog from the evening which a slight breeze had just failed to disperse completely. A little blue struggled through here and there in the dull, almost overcast sky

At breakfast, Kay had mentioned that Jacqueline had come down early and after a light breakfast of toast had driven off. He thought of his mother. He should really get to see her later that day. As for Jacqueline, he considered it important that they had met. She had acted as a stimulant to his almost latent desire to be a writer and a better artist. She had nudged him into a wider perspective with regards to his views and his interpretation of ideas and of visual images.

Sometimes, though rarely, events, emotions, people and even unseasonable weather may accidentally juxtapose to create a perfect moment. This moment would seldom be one of great drama or excitation. Its perfection would be in its simplicity.

Michael and Jacqueline had just been to a matinee performance of *The Three Sisters* in London and had walked the short distance to the Victoria Embankment Gardens. They sat on a bench and had the take-away coffee in its warm waxed paper cup from the nearby kiosk. There was the usual residue of heaviness of heart after a Chekov play. Michael had put his arm around her waist and she had rested her head on his shoulder and almost dozed off. The narrow gardens ran alongside the busy embankment and, although never completely free from the noise of the traffic, offered a quieter haven to rest in.

She opened her eyes to the shifting dazzle of the sun shimmering through the leaves of a large plane tree. She could feel the comforting nearness of Michael and heard the song of a common garden bird. That struck her as a perfect moment. She understood full well what the sisters might have felt if they had managed to get back to Moscow[1] – not the moment before nor the moment after – just the first flush of emotions. Perfect moments might not bear up to analysis.

A persistent mist veiled the town into the afternoon. Jacqueline looked around and saw Carl ruffling his hair, which had tumbled over his eyes as he bent over the fish and chips. All around, the trees, the buildings and the people moving slowly, formed an ashen, spectral backdrop. The two of them, sitting on a boulder in the river, seemed the only vibrant living things, closed in, together, in harmony. That, she knew, was another perfect moment. And yet, almost immediately, she felt uneasy.

'Have you thought again about contacting your father?' she asked.

'Yes, but I'm not going to. I think it's time I take stock of what I am and what I have and try to make some sense of it. The last seven or eight years I'd

---

[1] The sisters never moved back to Moscow – it was an unfulfilled dream

simply drifted, too lazy and scared to think about the future. I really want to make something of myself, Jacqueline,' he paused and collected himself before continuing. 'My girls are quite independent now and they are really happy in the Netherlands. My place is too small to accommodate both of them but they have Becchi's parents to stay with when they come to London. My mother seems content to carry on as she is. I think she has low expectation and is not disappointed with life except in me perhaps. So, I have only myself to improve.'

'I think you are fortunate, Carl. Many people stop developing around thirty – they get a job, settle down, have a family and get set in their ways and ideas. You are sprouting all over with green shoots,' she laughed at the cliché picture of it, 'but you must be ruthless and tend only the healthiest and most promising ones. Don't look so gloomy,' she remarked. 'You should be enthused.'

'I am, really, Jacqueline,' he insisted and managed a smile. He was unable to tell her that he would miss her when she left. He would hate to be thought soppy. The last few days had created an attachment between them out of proportion to the short time they had spent together. Their lives had been so different, so separate and, except for this chance meeting at *Llugwy View*, there was nothing to preposition one onto the other.

He would have liked to take her back to his room and make love to her. The first time he had her it was at her invitation, it was an act of compassion and friendship. It tempered a fresh, molten relationship into a firm though unrealistic bond. To manoeuvre her into the same situation again seemed opportunistic and would demean the original virtue – and might prove shamefacedly unsuccessful.

He straightened up and brushed the thought aside. Turning towards her, he asked, 'You and Michael, would things be OK?'

'They have to be, Carl. Michael is the only truly good and reliable thing in my life. The reality of love is full of negatives. It is almost inevitably elusive, misguided, unrealistic and disruptive. But Michael loves me – that is unquestionable. And that is strange because he is such a sensible and unsentimental person. I'd told myself before now that it is like Richard Dawkins[1] secretly believing in God – a real contradiction in terms,' she said and laughed.

'I needed some time away from him to think and understand and make my decision. I had no intension of enduring a marriage. I wanted to be sure that I wanted this marriage. I will try my hardest to make this work again. My one fear is that Michael might not be able to forgive himself for this lapse of judgment. And that would be my fault, Carl, for not being spontaneous enough from the very start to accept his sacrifice in corrupting his principles for love.'

She got up and suggested they went back.

---

[1] Oxford University Professor and author of many books including 'The Selfish Gene' and 'The God Delusion'

'I'm sorry there is little that I could say or help in this,' Carl said.

'Nonsense, Carl. You had been a Godsend. I have enjoyed being with you,' she said, placing her hands on his arms and kissing him on the cheek.

From her handbag she got out a postcard of some sheep on a rocky slope and handed it to Carl.

'You gave me a line on destiny etched in stone. In return I have only a presentiment written on paper,' she added, turning the card over.

> The rustle in my heart
> Warns of falling leaves
> Of lengthening shadows
> Of waning and abating
> Of ending and decaying

'That is rather grim,' Carl remarked, to which she made no comment.

'I'll go and see you at Pangbourne,' he added, before he lost courage

'You make sure you think about writing again. I'd love to call on your studio when you have completed your paintings of Snowdon. Well, we must get back. I don't want to be too late getting home.'

They walked briskly through the lifting fog back to *Llugwy.View*. He went sullenly upstairs to bring down her small travelling case and the backpack while she looked for Kay and Brian to say goodbye. He was despondent when he realized that he would not be alone with her to say a few last words, to cast a link however tenuous to the future, before she left.

Standing a little back with Kay and Brian, he saw her reverse her 2CV into the drive, turn right and drive into the distance towards another independent chapter of her life.

He was immediately lost and alone. He had been a vibrant character in a single short chapter of her life and that chapter had ended and the denouement had sped away without him. But he had gained so much. In her company, he told himself, he had been in a supporting role, but now he must embrace the role of the star and make of his life in the direction she had intimated.

5 Reaching Out

He could feel her hair resting against his neck and cheek. He thought she might know he was awake, but he was wary of opening his eyes, wary of having to respond in a situation he was unsure of.

She had come home early for she had missed him. When she saw him sleeping off the jet lag, she did not have the heart to wake him. She would cook pasta for dinner. She defrosted some prawns and put a bottle of dry Chilean white in the fridge. She went back to the bedroom, drew the long, wide, plain curtains so that it would be more restful and then lay beside him.

It was a luxury to be resting in bed on an afternoon and with Michael. She realized for the first time that she was actually tired, that it would be a good thing to take things easy sometimes. When you have been cocooned in the smug comfort of a satisfactory relationship, it is easy to stop thinking about it and about yourself, expecting life to dance sedately on in its usual mellow pace towards an expected happy end. But like heartbeats and breathing – you only notice them when there is discordance. And she noticed him –

the dark unshaven shadow on his face, the trace of freckles on his nose and cheeks, a few lines on his brow, which she had always thought so even. For the first time in years, she noticed him as a separate entity from her, from the oneness of their marriage. There was freshness in her feelings towards him, a fresh requirement.

Michael turned around and put an arm around her. 'What time is it?' he asked, noticing the drawn curtains.

'Not quite 5. I came home early,' she explained. 'You look exhausted.'

'I had not slept very well while away. I find the great cities of China all-consuming – millions of people constantly on the move, constantly eating, constantly shopping, constantly manufacturing, and endlessly polluting the air. You can't help being charged by all the energy around you. You are energized and then you suddenly realized you had almost everything sucked out of you.

These ever growing cities should be the vital organs of the country, enriching it, regulating it, refreshing it and making it whole and great. Instead, I fear they might be like cancerous growths that would vacuum in all the goodness from around them, become their own raison d'être, leaving the country desperate. China is at a turning point and it needs a great visionary leader to transform it. But I bore.'

'Nonsense. I love listening to you. I thought you loved china.'

'How can one help but to love or hate being in China. In the cities you are invigorated by a maelstrom of activities that inevitably draws you in. Then you take a train journey through the Provinces to visit a factory or for a meeting and what you see astound you. The different pace of life, the harmony of the landscape with the lifestyle of small farmers, the serenity, all help to calm you down. There the grandeur of nature dwarfs mankind. In the cities, nature has been assigned to a few gardens and public parks. China leaves me giddy and confused.'

'I'd love to go to China,' she said.

'We'll go. We'll find the time. You need time to get to grip with China. It's not just the ancient history and the great scenery which you see on TV and films. These are only the static backdrops to a great sociological experience. There'll be things like dirt and some strange food they enjoy which you'll absolutely hate. But you'll love the people, their aspiration and drive. Everyone appears to be hungry for some just out of reach goal.'

He questioned if they would be happy there. The wonderment of discovering new places, the startlement each time of finding that they resonated with each other, were affected by colours and sounds and textures in the same way and even where they disagreed they understood the other's point of view – could all these truly exist within the milieu of his guilt? He looked at her, stifled a sigh, and smiled reassuringly.

She looked at her watch and moved to get up to get dinner, but he held her back gently by the arm and asked her about her trip to Wales.

'It went exceedingly well,' she replied. 'I'd had lots of time to think and to understand.'

Michael sat up and looked searchingly at her. That was not the end of the story, he told himself. Nothing was ever so simple with Jacqueline. And he would not have had it any differently. It would be intolerable to have to live grounded with someone with a plain mind and a lack of imagination. She bore wings and he had always aspired to soar in accompaniment.

'I went up Snowdon with Carl who had the other room on the top floor at the back, across from my room, remember? We spent some time together. Carl is sort of an artist who has a small art gallery somewhere near Earls Court. His real drive is to be a writer. We had some interesting chat about that,' she concluded.

Ah, an artist, he thought. That didn't surprise him – someone creative, someone who could accommodate the agile twist and turn of her mind. A cerebral contortionist, he spitted.

'And was he able to get you out of the wood?'

'I am here aren't I, Michael?'

'Did he fuck you?' he asked softly.

'You were not there,' she replied, not as an excuse, nor an accusation, but as an explanation. 'I had so much on my mind. I needed to make sure the decision I made was a sound and correct one. I was wrought with misgivings and needs and I had to get the monkey off my back to see my way clearly.' Then she laughed.

'I had to instigate it. I am not quite his type, I don't think.'

She reached out and held his hand.

'Come now, darling, we'll see our way ahead, together,' she said.

It was a fine September evening. The setting sun behind the house lit up the hills beyond the valley opposite and the high, wispy cirrus clouds caught a little of its gold. Michael strummed on his guitar as Jacqueline brought up a tray of coffee and the unfinished bottle of wine from dinner to the balcony. Sitting there, in their own home, with a view of almost lyrical beauty, in the quiet freshness of the countryside broken only occasionally by the cooing of returning pigeons to their roosts among the trees, and with the familiar strum of Michael at the guitar, she felt settled. If it was how their lives had finally come together and how it would end, there could be no complaint. Time had been kind in filtering away the dregs and leaving behind it this gentle fineness of love and tranquillity.

For a long while she did not speak, savouring this feeling of calm, afraid it might simply be an illusion, whose fragility might shatter at a whisper.

'When did you say Josh is getting married?' Michael asked, at a tangent.

'Last week in October. I have the date and details in my diary.'

'I must say I'm a little surprised.'

'Why?

'He seems to me rather careful.'

'They have been together over 4 years,' Jacqueline added.

'Even then a little rash for Josh.'

'I am not aware that you have an opinion on him.'

Not an opinion. I don't know him well enough – just an impression.'

'I thought we'll get him a good coffee machine,' she said.

'Is that something he needs?' Michael asked.

'It's something he wanted. Denise passed me his gift list.'

'Well I never.'

'I'm afraid we are rather passé, you know. People are more into gadgets than we are. And there are more of them about. I'll also write a cheque from the company.'

Michael looked at her and mused at the word 'passé'.

'I suppose we'd never been with it,' he commented.

It wasn't till May the following year that Carl finally took the train to Pangbourne. This created an oasis in what was by then an arid and dispirited juncture in her life. It was a breathing space, a watering place. She had wondered whether he would contact her when he had completed his painting of Snowdon but, as time passed, it had lost its immediacy and significance and she thought no more of it.

When he appeared at the office so unexpectedly, she was caught with an unguarded pleasure, simple, undiluted and innocent. 'This is my friend Carl,' she introduced him to Josh and Denise and to David who was just leaving.

Carl had taken his mother to the Netherlands for Christmas as promised. The previous months had been hectic as his gallery prepared for the Christmas and New Year season. They had selected and offered a small sales range and introduced sales vouchers. After the New Year he had to organize and display twenty paintings from two London artists with the city as the theme.

As the result of its success, he was approached by several other artists to display their works. The size of the gallery limited what he could accept, but there was a water-colourist whose portfolio he admired and he made several visits to his workshop to plan for a display later in the spring.

As for his own work, he had completed two pictures in oil from his early sketches in Wales. One was of three sheep on a craggy hillside and another of a stone cottage by a boulder strewn stream. They were pretty enough and decorative enough above a mantelpiece or in place of a large mirror in an apartment sitting room, but he could find no soul in them.

He had delayed looking at the sketch he made at *Cwm Clogwyn* because he wanted the final painting to reflect not only what he felt but also to evoke his brief, significant encounter with Jacqueline. It should have not only a visual impact but be viscerally exciting. She had been shunted momentarily, with occasional twinges of conscience on his part, to one side. He could not function with her on his mind.

In March, however, he came across the postcard Jacqueline had given him with:

> The rustle in my heart
> Warns of falling leaves
> Of lengthening shadows
> Of waning and abating
> Of ending and decaying

There was desolation, anticipation and even a hint of fear in it. He wondered how she was and how she and Michael had got on. He looked at his sketch book again and it brought back to him the colours, the forms and the emotion he had felt that day at the edge of *Cwm Clogwyn*. That weekend he stayed in and started to work on the picture. The result after two weeks was not exactly the masterpiece he had intended. He knew it would take a great artist to create on canvas what the mind had visualized, but he also knew he was but a mediocre painter.

The foreground contained areas of rich tones in the variegated colours of the mosses and rocks. This contrasted effectively with the intruding white and blueish grey fog, sombre in parts, but tinged at the top right corner with a broken splash of peachy hopefulness. As an after-thought he painted a slate pebble at the bottom right hand corner with his initials on it.

He called the finished picture '… *if fate will have me king'*. The title was obscure, apparent only to Jacqueline and him, but as he intended to keep it, it made no odds. He decided that Jacqueline would not judge it too harshly and planned to take a photo of it, surprise her with it at Pangbourne and invite her to London to view it at his flat.

On various trips to Oxford and the Midlands on the train, Carl had passed Pangbourne but had never had reason to stop over. This time he got off and simply followed five fellow passengers towards the centre of the small town. He walked past *Accent Recruitment* but courage failed him. He looked around the town, walked across the bridge over the Thames into Whitchurch before turning back and ended up having a coffee on the terrace of the *George Hotel*.

What Carl found difficult to cope with in any relationship were the beginning and the ending of it. He was never certain enough of himself to make quick decisions on how to approach a new situation or to make a break from it when it had come to a natural deadlock. He was most comfortable in the organic duration when events took natural turns and twists without efforts on his part. He was unusually bashful about imposing himself on Jacqueline. But, he told himself, it would be futile to guess at her possible reactions. He should just drink up the coffee and drop in on her.

'Just say it's a friend,' he told Naomi the receptionist. He wanted an element of surprise and to see what her spontaneous reaction was. Her response did not disappoint him. He immediately felt comfortable. After introducing him to Josh, she explained to David about their meeting in Wales and, since David was about to leave, she asked Carl into her office.

'I must make a couple of calls and finish this report,' she beamed. 'It won't take long and then we could get out of here'. She handed him a copy of that day's *Daily Telegraph* and proceeded to make her calls. Denise knocked on the door and enquired if either of them would like a coffee. Jacqueline shook her head and looked at Carl who turned to Denise and said no.

Carl did not question her warmth and joy at seeing him. He concluded that she was really free from artifice. There was no embarrassing silence or hesitation in her response. When he first saw Josh and David, he realized how foolish it was of him not to have anticipated that Michael might also be there. The thought had not entered his mind. He knew though that if Michael had been there, Jacqui would have acted in exactly the same way. Her simple reaction somehow negated any significance that he might have attributed to what had happened in Wales.

Lunch was at *Style Acre* through ten miles of beautiful Downlands [1] of West Berkshire and South

---

[1] Gently rolling hills especially in Southern England

Oxfordshire to the village of Blewbury [1]. Situated within the grounds of *Savages*, a small garden centre cum farm shop, *Style Acre* was a favourite haunt of Jacqueline's. It offered breakfast and cakes in the morning and, later in the day, a selection of freshly prepared sandwiches, Panini, jacket potatoes and simple dishes of the day. Run by the charity *Style Acre* which supported adults with learning difficulties, helping them gain independence and introducing them to the working environment, the restaurant was unpretentious, serving good, fresh food with a large serving of warmth and country friendliness. Carl had never seen anything like it. They both ordered jacket potatoes and coffees and as it was a warm, sunny day, they sat outside under a small marquee.

Living in London suited Carl and his business but every time he left for the country, he was dazed and dazzled by the change. It was like he had broken through an invisible barrier into new worlds, each impacting him in a different way. The uplands of Wales and Scotland, with their crags and steep rocky slopes generated in him a passion, a wild force of nature so strong that he was filled with a sense of untenable emotional longing. While walking along the coast, be it tracing the edge of long lines of cliffs, listening to the roar of the waves carousing against the rocks, or along a quiet, docile beach, he would feel

---

[1] Kenneth Grahame, author of The Wind In The Willows, lived at Blewbury before moving to Pangbourne

most his loneliness for he associated the coast with romance, with a woman by his side, with nature's generative call.

And here, the gentle, undulating, farmed landscape, with its variegated crops, its copses and hedgerows, instilled in him a mellowness and a calm that is civilized. On the surface there was nothing that would ruffle. Even the dazzling yellow fields of rapeseed plants[1] seemed to have acquired their niche. Here man had embraced the land, had husbanded it, considerate to each party's mutual needs. One should feel assured, comfortable, moderated. Things were managed. Emotions were managed. Appearances were managed. This was truly a temperate land.

The country road rolled along like a dragon's back and from the top of each roll, he exclaimed, he could see an orgy of farms stretching into the distance, one on top of the other. At a distance, Jacqueline pointed out, was *Wittenham Clumps*[2], two significant chalk hills crowned with clumps of beech trees – a local landmark and nature reserve which had inspired Paul Nash, the artist.

'I remember your saying in Wales that you couldn't live a life that is mediocre. What could seem more mediocre than what you could see here? Everything is toned down. However, I believe you feel the vibes of

---

[1] Canola plants

[2] Wittenham Clumps is managed by Earth Trust and has association with the artist Paul Nash, who did several paintings of it.

227

what seethes beneath the surface, something deep down. Something more intoxicating than it appears. Nothing that human hands had touched is ever quite simple. I think one's reaction reflects one's personal nature. You have a sensitive and responsive nature. I think I have just complimented you.'

Over coffee at *Style Acre* she enquired the timing of his visit.

'There's a time for everything and I thought it is the appropriate time. We'd been busy at the gallery and I had found it impossible to start on this until recently,' he handed her the photo of his painting of *Cwm Clogwy*. 'I didn't quite know if you'd really welcome my visit. I wanted to see you and so I came and was prepared to face the consequences,' he continued.

'Well, I'm pleased to see you. You've cropped your hair,' she added.

'I decided it had become redundant. Something you said in Wales made me think that an artist needs not sport long hair and a writer needs not forever look pensive. So here I am, looking rather droll and exposed.'

'I like it. The essential man – nothing wrong with that. Now, why did you find it so difficult to start on this painting?

'Wales, I think. When we had climbed Snowdon, I thought, I had done this so many times. I knew the country around. It was beautiful. I enjoyed the exertion and the sense of well-being after I had come down. It gave me a sense of freedom from the daily grind of work and living in London. Doing it more leisurely with you this time, it occurred to me that there was a similarity between it and how I had lived my life. It had its ups and downs, its moments of joy and sadness, its successes and failures. But never had I slowed down to think about it as a whole and question who I was, where I was heading and why.

It was a long, jumbled up and tedious passage without structure or cohesion. Then you came along and for no apparent reason I could find, helped me to insert the commas and full stops, question marks and exclamation marks. I began to collate and to paragraph. I began to think and to understand myself better. When it came to painting this picture, I wanted so much that it be good or at least up to a standard I was capable of producing. I was afraid to fail your trust in me but more significantly, I was afraid to fail me.'

'I am not a qualified judge, but I like this very much. I had expected there to be much more obvious passion in your strokes and use of colours. There is instead restraint and maturity – a much more elevated quality to achieve. Where the fog encroaches the moss and the rocks there is this contrast of water-colour softness against the strength of oil. Yet the overall picture is one of wholesomeness. I really do like it,' Jacqui said and handed the photo back to Carl.

'Dare I hope that you would come to London and see it? I painted it in my flat and it is still there.'

'I'd love to. Wednesday's usually a good day for me although I could get away most days. Josh has taken over much of my work and he now calls on prospective clients. I'm lucky to have somebody I have confidence in – someone sensible. You'll like Josh,' she added.

They finished lunch around 2 o'clock and Jacqui drove to *Wittenham Clumps*. From the small car park, they walked up a gentle grassy slope to the wooded clump of *Castle Hill*, an Iron-age hill fort where the ditch and part of the rampart are still visible. On a clear, sunny day in late spring or summer, Jacqui insisted, there is no place more pleasant or charming than the English countryside.

The wood is mainly of beech trees and there is a trace of a trampled path through it. They strayed from the path deeper into the wood where ankle deep crisp fallen leaves from the previous autumn had collected. Here and there hardy brambles had already pushed their way through and further along nearer the edge, curls of young bracken had broken with vitality into the semi shade.

It did not take long for the eyes to adjust from the bright and strident sunshine outside to the soothing bower below the trees. Looking up, Carl could see the canopy of diverse shades of green emanating from eager, young leaves casting a cool translucence around them. There remained a slight mustiness which, no doubt, the onset of summer would dissipate. Now and again there was tweeting from some hidden chaffinches, but most birds had done with their morning songs.

'This always moves me,' Jacqui said, 'the juxtaposition of crinkly dead leaves on the ground from one year with the new shoots of life of the next. It is the tale of life – not of an individual life but of the continuity of life. You and I are links along that chain. We are important too this short, short while we are here.'

She ran her right hand over the weathered trunk of a beech tree and, bending down, she picked up an armful of the crisp, dry leaves and lifting them slightly, tossed them upwards over her head and, as they fell, cited:

Ah! As the heart grows older
It will come to such sights colder
By and by, nor spare a sigh
Though Worlds of wanwood leafmeal lie[1]

'Hopkins,' she explained and spoke a little about it and of Gerald Manley Hopkins as they strolled out of the wood. They went along a field of young cereal till they reached a breach and turned off along a wide path bordered by further woodlands. When they reached the top of the *Round Hill*, she pointed out the village of *Little Wittenham, Dorchester-on-Thames*, the *River Thames* and where the *Poohsticks Bridge*[2] was.

---

[1] Gerard Manley Hopkins – Spring and Fall

[2] A footbridge across the Thames where the World Poohsticks Championship used to be held. The event has now been moved to Witney in Oxfordshire

It was a still afternoon. The sun angled down from a Westerly direction. It was a mid-week mid-afternoon and the few post-lunch dog walkers had gone off home. She felt him turning to look at her. In the crisp dryness, as she turned to face him, there was a frisson of the imminent, of the kindling of a tinder dry life.

He felt an inevitability. He took her in his arms and very gently kissed her. There was no hurry. There was no prowess to prove. Lying on his light jacket on the dry grass, they made love. It was not an earth moving, soul shattering experience for either of them but an acceptance of each other into their lives.

'South Oxfordshire has never been confronted by such an absurd sight,' she laughed.

They had not deemed it inappropriate nor were they shamefaced as they walked back to the car in silence, his arm around her waist.

'You know what? I shall come and see you next Wednesday,' she proposed and he accepted.

Jacqui did not place much importance to casual sexual encounters. These were to her just paraphernalia of life. She had never asked nor even been interested in whether Michael had had casual affairs on his trips abroad. If they were of significance, she trusted that he would have told her about them. That she had made love with Carl in Wales was, to her, simply utilitarian. It was a one-off. It happened and ended in situ. It left no trail nor made forward waves.

But this new relationship put her in a quandary. By nature she would need to tell Michael about it and to sit down and discuss it. They had to talk about their relationship and in which direction it should or could be going. What had gone wrong between them she could not grapple with, add to, subtract from or formulate a solution to. Michael's problems were psychologically self-imposed. He was as defenceless as she was helpless in dealing with them.

She was determined to be there to support him and uphold their marriage. But she could not possibly tell him, who was down and guilt-ridden, that she was involved with someone else. It would add to his humiliation, his measure of worthlessness, his appropriation of blame and guilt. She could not do that to him. She needed to be strong for both of them. In order to be so, she needed this escape, this coping mechanism.

To be fair to Carl, she had to like him and appreciate and value him in order to be involved. She enjoyed his company and was interested in his artistic development. She could contribute to his growth as a person. Michael and she were an establishment, undermined and faltering at its foundation, but stable enough yet, salvageable yet. Carl and she were not an item. She felt she could be his support, perhaps even be his guide. Carl, however, must be the master of his own creation.

When there is no immediate need to get out of a quandary, it is often convenient to remain in its grip. For the time being, Jacqueline was willing to let things be.

There is no thrill like the thrill of waiting for the imminent arrival of an illicit lover. It is not like waiting for a spouse, or a partner. It is not a duty or an obligation and is not enveloped within the tyranny of social circumspection. It has a simple purpose. The downside of it is that when the day is over and that purpose is fulfilled, that eagerly awaited lover might become an intrusion into your space. Your freedom becomes curtailed. You can't function for want of air. One of you should get out and it ought not to be you. How to be tactful? Would one wished to retain the relationship? Is the relationship worth retaining? Could one be rude and ask the just-been lover to get lost? That would be hurtful. Back to circumspection. Grin and bear it.

Waiting outside Sloane Square tube station, Carl experienced a new kind of thrill, of excitement. More than a lover, Jacqui was to him a source, a mirror. How could she be an intrusion when she was the spatial spectrum into which he wanted to roam and cull and absorb? He enjoyed listening to her and valued her opinions.

In her absence, he couldn't quite visualize her. She was an impression, a suggestion, an outline, but a definition escaped him. And then suddenly there she was. In the open country of Snowdon there was drama in her look, her moves, and her stature. But here, outside a London tube station with hundreds of milling

Lowryish[1] figures and persistent, strident traffic noise, she paled and diminished into just another commuter, another matchstick. She was nothing special to look at. Not a triumphant trophy to strut alongside with. But there she was, and it filled him with joy.

They stopped at a local café for a quick sandwich before walking the half mile to his first floor flat. The flat was in a block of six late Victorian terrace houses. The exterior still preserved the slightly fussy features of the time but once through the door with its ornate upper stained glass panel, the interior had been modernised and converted into a small basement flat with two more above it.

Jacqueline was surprised at how spacious the open plan living area appeared to be. There was a bay window at the front and a large window at the back giving much light to the kitchen area. There was a large bedroom at the front and a box room behind it. The bathroom was adjacent to the kitchen but opening from the living area. A small dining table with just three chairs suggested to her that Carl hardly entertained at home. But the sitting area was comfortable.

Carl went to open each window in the house before getting back to her and offering her a drink. There was a persistent smell of oil paint in the house which he tried to get rid of. Besides, it was a habit he had inherited from his grandmother. 'Make sure your room

---

[1] Reference to Laurence Stephen Lowry's paintings with matchstick men figures

is aired, Carl,' she would say to him when he came home from school. 'Get some fresh air in, love,' she would add. Ever since, he had equated a closed room with stale and stagnant air until he had left the windows open for a while. Then he could operate. Then he could think.

The painting he wanted to show her was standing on an easel in the dining area. He had covered it with a dust sheet to reveal it when he was ready.

Judging from the photograph Carl had given her, Jacqueline had expected a much larger canvas. The painting was closer to an A1[1] size and sat well within the living area. She decided that Carl was not as good a photographer as he was an artist. There was so much more depth in the actual painting than indicated in the photograph. The fog appears to advance and loom towards the viewer. Behind the seemingly soft and white fog hid ominous shades of greys. One immediately felt an oncoming force which would soon envelop the brighter, harsher and more solid mosses, grass and stones. There was a glow to the top right of the fog. The first response was that it was a sign of hope filtering through. But no, it was a reflection. Soon the fog could encroach on the sun's domain or could the sun stem the fog's progress? To someone who knew the spot, there was also the knowledge of the danger beyond the fog. There was that sharp rocky drop of the Cwm.

---

[1] A1 – 23.4″ x 33.1″ or 594mm x 841mm

On a non-prominent piece of flat slate at the bottom right corner, Jacqueline could just make out the suggestion of '*If fate will have me king*' and his initials. At first she considered it a conceit, but was then persuaded that it was in fact the summation of the picture.

The uncertainty of nature and of life, the strife between the dark and the light, the pointlessness of human hopes and despair when it was chance which was the key player and final determiner. She was moved by the nuances in what was after all a landscape painting. It was an understated depiction of the vagaries of existence.

She turned to Carl and said, 'I like it very much.'

It was as if for the first time she saw him as a grown man, a man with a brain within his body, a man with prospect to be a good artist and perhaps an even better writer. A man worth having known. So few. There really had been so few.

Years later, whenever he had received praise on one of his paintings or a critical acclaim for a book, he would always look back to this moment when Jacqueline had simply said 'I like it very much'. It was packed with all that was unsaid and he knew that therein lay the kernel of her praise. And he would wonder what she would have thought of it.

He first made love to her in Wales at her request, as an accomplice. At *Wittenham Clumps*, he mused, it was circumstantial. The surroundings, the weather, the poetry of their proximity all conspired towards a sexual encounter. But on that day he was at his home ground. There arose in him that hunter's instinct of landing a prey. That male prerogative of dominance and possession overpowered him. He did not consider courtesy nor possible rejection. Her took her in his arms, kissed her with his force and carried her to his bed.

Never had a woman yielded and acquiesced so knowledgeably to his every demand and lust. He felt the master. He felt the conqueror. He lay exhausted beside her and thought, 'There would be other women. Awaiting me there must be just as exciting sex and pleasure as this. But I know Jacqueline would remain the most significant experience in my life.'

He turned to look at her – her eyes closed and her smile content – and suddenly he felt, heh! I have been outmanoeuvred here.

Carl had no illusion about this affair. He knew that one day, not too far ahead, it was bound to end. If she were kind, she would explain why and there would be a tearful parting on each side. It would also not surprise him if she would just walk away with no explanation, expecting him to know and understand that there could be only Michael in her life. He hoped they had a little more time left. He was in no hurry to pursue his future. He would write. He would succeed. She had engendered in him the will to be – to be whatever he wished to be within his capabilities. He was thankful.

Edward once told Jacqueline, 'Youth and inexperience don't keep a man. You made a God of Gérard and off he went. You gave him your love and off he went. You needed him and he didn't care two hoots. A man stays if HE thinks he needed you. A man stays if HE thinks he is fascinated by you. He wants an illusion not reality. It's all in his bloody mind. It's never what you are but what you made him think you are that is crucial. It is hard work keeping a man. Is it worth the trouble, Jacqueline? I don't know. Go and discover, learn and then ask that question. Only you could answer it. But for goodness sake never become stale, for when you have, you will bore even yourself.

Well, she thought, *youth* certainly no longer qualified her. She and Michael had settled into a pattern of life but she could not say that they were bored with each other. All she had experienced, however, had not made her any clearer or even wiser. And here she was *experiencing* again.

The problem with experiencing was that it usually involved other people's lives and one had to be fair – but one wasn't – not often. Of Carl, she had little worries. He was a survivor. He was a man with a mission and she was just an encounter en route. It excited her that she was part of his adventure – of his worthy adventure towards being a writer, towards being a more profound being, a more sensitive and perceptive being.

'Ah!' she sighed, 'to be the prism that could broadcast the colours of his life.'

From a bedside drawer, Carl brought out a small gift-wrapped box for her. He must be pretty certain of his success with her, she thought, to have a gift ready by the bed. Or, 'does every woman get a gift at the end of a session?' she asked, laughing.

'There aren't that many sessions and no, sex has nothing to do with it,' he retorted.

She untied the fine gold ribbon and removed the black paper wrapping that some nimble fingers must have put together so deftly. From the size of it she guessed it could be a piece of jewellery or a bottle of perfume, either of which could be tricky. Please Lord, she thought, don't let it be a bottle of cheap perfume that she had to pretend to like and worse, to actually wear.

'Ah,' she whispered, as she opened the classic white box, 'Chanel 5.'

'Is that OK?' he asked hesitatingly.

'Perfect,' she replied in amazement. 'How did you know that's what I wear?'

He put an arm around her and turning round kissed her.

'I have a good nose,' he said, his eyes twinkling with impish mischief. 'You know how a piece of music reminds some people of people and places and events? Perfume has the same effect on me. It is so special that I had never given perfume to anyone else besides my wife. I want always to be reminded of you. And perhaps, it would sometimes remind you of me, I hope,' he added.

Walking into *John Lewis*[1] a couple of days earlier, he had stopped by a perfume counter and wondered. It had to be French. Something classic and not a fad. Something mellow. Something that would suggest but not shout. Definitely a perfume and not an eau de toilette. He narrowed them down to Dior or Chanel. He had mentioned all these to the woman assistant at the counter, who was mature enough to appreciate such subtleties. After just four samplings he closed his eyes and pictured her and decided on Chanel 5. It was only a small 25ml bottle. Nothing ostentatious. And with her in his arms, in his bed, he felt warm with pride for having spotted it correctly.

Jacqueline turned around and he kissed her again.

'If you're up to it Carl..,' she whispered.

'Need you ask?'

And she urged him on.

She had laid low the balance and drew a veil over the lady's eyes[2]. She would think about Michael and of justice later on. For the first time she felt the bile of Michael's injustice towards her. She had tried to salvage a perfectly fine ship that simply wouldn't float. She had been patient and supportive and had borne no ill-feeling towards him for his mistakes. To continue to do so she needed strength – a strength which at that

---

[1] A departmental Store

[2] Blind-folded Lady Justice holding the balance

moment Carl could generate. Justice? She would think of it later. Morality? She could only sustain the morality and duty of survival. Don't look towards morality and religion for comforting answers cast in stone. Go there for a debate and try to win, Edward had said. She would think more about the situation later. Not just then.

Carl took her to the underground. He had agreed to return to Pangbourne the following week for her to show him the bluebell woods on a stretch of the *Ridgeway*. In this fashion they continued to meet for just five more times over the next two months. They lunched sometimes at *Nino's*[1] in Pangbourne or at the *Bull at Streatley*. They walked on the *Holies* and at *Lardon Chase*[2] with its panoramic views of Streatley and Goring before crossing the Thames to have coffee at the *Goring Café*. How could he ever forget those afternoons spent in West Berkshire and South Oxfordshire? And there is a lasting warmth in his heart in remembering both of them, sitting by the Thames, so tranquil, drinking in each other's vibes of affection at *Don Giovanni* at the edge of Goring. Towards the end of July, she rang him and asked, 'Shall I come up to you on Wednesday?'

---

[1] Family run Italian Restaurant now on Reading Road, but many years ago was at the back of The George Hotel

[2] The Holies and Lardon Chase are adjacent National Trust properties on the edge of Berkshire Downs above Streatley-on-Thames.

They met at *The Tate Modern* at mid-morning and had breakfast. Carl walked her round the exhibits and explained why he liked certain pieces or paintings. Current modern art was not a milieu she was knowledgeable or enamoured with but she understood the virtue of silence in ignorance and of respect for Carl's revelation. As he explained a particular painting to her, her eyes welled with tears with missing Michael. She turned away a little and asked if they could go back to his flat. She took his hand to show that he had not offended or displeased her, but did not explain her tears.

There were possible reasons he could think of, but she left him with those possibilities. He knew it was that unfathomable and unpossessable quality in her that would possess and mystify him for the rest of his life. It was, each time, somehow about her. He was always the accessory. She belonged elsewhere, but for moments he had her.

Oh, Jacqueline, that last time he saw her, as she walked away at the corner of the street, like a mirage, into the haze of an after rain London. She would not let him accompany her to the underground. She wanted her last memory of him to be the warmth of him. He walked a short distance with her and then, with umbrella in her hand she mingled with the crowd. At any moment he almost expected her to flick open the umbrella and then up, up into the sky, never to return

Mid-August was not a time they would normally go to France. The French went on their holidays then. Restaurants and chambres d'hôtes[1] were often closed and neither Michael nor Jacqueline liked the stifling heat of some still summer days in Champagne. But Michael wanted a fighting chance – a last fighting chance. He needed them to get away to somewhere familiar where they had been happy. Somewhere to discover if they had anything left to re-discover.

He was told about Carl's frequent visits to Pangbourne, usually on a Wednesday. He had feigned disinterest for he considered his personal life strictly private. He was given a little more details but he would not pursue it. What would be the purpose of it? Feed and fuel the eager engine of gossips? What could he do? He would not rant nor scream nor strike out. Besides, this would not have happened if he had not failed her.

He had for some time considered alternatives and, that Jacqueline might have a chance of happiness elsewhere, made it imperative that they should find opportunities soon to discuss the matter. He had to swipe clean that slate of guilt hidden in his psyche that had disempowered him of all sexual prowess – unfocussed desires that dissipated in execution. He had become the embodiment of the meaningless man. A

---

[1] Bed and Breakfasts

Hollow man[1]. A King gone fishing[2]. What was he to expect of an unattended realm?

Deep down in the landscape of his mind, there had been a single dislocated tremor that had caused disproportionate trauma on the surface which had disorientated him. Michael is lost, he mused. Other men would just get on with it and make the best of the situation, but he had lost the facility. You don't command a paralysed man to just get up and get on with it because other men could. But he must give it another try.

They left Reims early and stopped over at Epernay where they bought a small case of local wine, a baguette, half a smoked chicken, a jar of rillettes de porc and a pack of remoulade de céleri[3]. Jacqueline had mentioned how she would like to go back to the restaurant *Mont Aimé* at Bergères-lès-Vertus, so he made a detour and they had lunch there. He loved doing little favours for her because they were so seldom requested. The restaurant had not changed much and she was pleased to find the Îles flottantes[4] à la maison still on the menu.

They talked a little about when they were last there about ten years ago in September. Jacqueline told him about her stay at a vineyard in the Loire valley during

---

[1] Reference to T S Eliot – The Hollow Men

[2] Reference to the Arthurian Legends of The Fisher King

[3] Remoulade of celeriac

[4] Floating Islands, a classic French dessert of soft meringue floating in crème anglaise

the vendanges many years ago, not long before she first met him. These were things of the past, but at least they were talking and laughing and perhaps beginning to enjoy each other's presence – something so simple but so difficult to initiate when so much contrary lay within each one's mind.

She noticed the light freckles on his nose and knew that in a day or two they would spread to his cheeks. She liked them. They lent a little quirkiness and added a little flaw to his looks. They gave him character. She had no time for pretty, meaningless faces. Some of the most structurally beautiful people lose their charm on acquaintance. Michael always came alive when he spoke and even in silence he spoke to her. The beginning of a smile; the slight frown; an eye-brow raised and held or dropped; the twinkling or dimming of the eyes; that lean hunger; that wry but cheeky grin. Oh, she knew him so well. But then, lately, he spoke to her only of negativity; of despondency.

Later, at the chambre d'hôte, he heard her open the bathroom door and he opened his eyes. He could see her standing still for a moment, adjusting to the darkened room, before approaching slowly.

'Come here,' he called. He wanted to clear his mind of Jacqueline the known quantity and to take her as a woman, any woman. He was incapable as yet of balancing his psyche on the tightrope of their relationship. He was a man in raw need of a woman. Perhaps if he could take her successfully without the usual analysis, they might stand a chance. But first, he had to forget his ego. Let go, let go of that grip he had on himself. They each had to abandon the very structure of their consciousness, forget the intrinsic knowledge they had of each other and made love as of the very first time.

They skipped supper. Jacqueline – lying there, a glass of wine in one hand, body spent, mind white hot with hopes, the other hand grasping his, for fear of letting go.

Michael – once again questioning the purpose of it all. Exciting sex could be bought or had around any corner of one's life. Comfortable sex with the person you loved and respected and understood was something he had with Jacqueline but which was somehow no longer attainable. This mental gymnastics and role-play required to fulfil their physical needs indicated the failure rather than the culmination of their relationship. To have to whore his own wife after almost thirty years of marriage was a level he had sunk to. He did not feel elated. He did not feel the high. There was only one way out. He had thought about it for some time, even before he had found out about Carl. Perhaps it was the time to discuss Carl with Jacqueline.

He had no idea how serious or otherwise the affair was. In a way he was disappointed that Jacqueline had not been open about Carl. The crux of the matter was that he had lost that special rapport, that intimacy of mind and body with Jacqueline. What happened between her and Carl was extraneous and existed only in the void that he had created. He did not credit it with much significance. Yet, he knew he had to go away. He could envisage, if he were to stay, a future of cordial indifference, of irritability and annoyance which would end in dislike for each other. These feeble emotions he despised.

He could endure her hatred, her anger, violent eruptions of frustrations, something on a scale of grandeur, but to be able to generate only feeble emotions he would find despicable. He could not allow himself to stay in this eventual internecine love affair.

The sun rose hazily and was still quite low above the rolling vineyards when she prepared coffee and they sat on the terrace. She had told the landlady that they would give breakfast a miss. She appeared to be in high spirits and tucked heartily into the rillettes de porc and the baguette. Michael kept to the baguette and coffee and opened a bottle of Bouzy rouge. Jacqueline had offered to do the driving that day so that he could enjoy his drinks.

He had reserved a table at *Chez Max* at Epernay for lunch and he hoped they could walk along the Marne afterwards. It was Michael's intention to break the news of his leaving then. He also needed to know about her relationship with Carl. If she had some emotional support from Carl when he left he would not feel as guilty. No more guilt for him. He needed his guilt lifted not compounded. For the moment he was never more in love with her and the knowledge that he had failed and had to leave pained him keenly. But he wanted to savour the present, the tableau and sensation they had wilfully created, and to take away with him this memory of Jacqueline and him sitting so cosily on a terrace, somewhere in France.

When the time came, he could not make himself open up to Jacqueline. They walked along the left bank of the Marne, often past houses and vineyards, but occasionally with views over the vineyards onto the river. Where there were shades from trees, they might stop a little, sat on a bench or on a grassy bank for some respite from the sun. It was not till the evening back in their room that he turned around to her in bed and said, ' I know about Carl,' and stopped.

'Ah,' she exclaimed and stopped, but accepting that the ball was then fairly in her court. She did not ask how he knew about Carl, assuming that such things usually got talked about. David might have let it slip, or either Josh or Denise had inadvertently mentioned it. In a way it made it easier for her to explain the situation to Michael.

'Carl came to see me at the office one day in March. We had not been in touch since I left Wales. You see, he had been doing these sketches of Snowdonia and he wanted to show me a picture of one of the finished paintings. He could have emailed it to me or put it in the post. I presumed he wanted to see me again. When I got back from Wales, I really wanted us to have a fresh start. I had decided that there was nothing to blame you or forgive you for. You did what you had to do for your survival and for me and I respected that.

But I grew rather listless and passive. Nothing felt quite the same between us since I got back from Wales. Was it because of Carl?' she asked.

'He had nothing to do with it. If things had been OK between us he would not have happened. I am not concerned with Carl. I am mad that I have been so inadequate that you had to go elsewhere,' he retorted in frustration.

'Well, Carl is history now. I stopped seeing him weeks ago. But I must make it clear that I have much respect and affection for him or I would not have allowed a relationship to grow. He is a creative and intelligent man. I hope that he will be successful in his art and writing. It was the right time for him for me to come along. He was aware always, I am certain, that my place will always be with you. I knew his strength and his weakness and I knew that when the time came he would understand that I had to go. In that respect I have been lucky. Neither of you are people who create scenes. I would hate that, won't you?'

'Some people might think we are wimps. Undramatic,' Michael suggested.

'Many people would, I'm sure. People need expansive gestures to demonstrate very little,' she added. She thought of her parents. Her mother with her classy Bostonian upbringing – quietly charming, non-assertive, minimal in gestures, bearing up with her father's garrulous, often unreasonable behaviour. Her father – not necessarily loud, but full of tales of his travels and West Country yarns – righteous and demanding of his wife as of a man's rights. Though not often at home, he expected a home conforming to his ideals waiting for him when he did return.

'Yes, I think I have been lucky in you,' she said.

'Jacqueline, what I am going to say is very difficult. I have been happy these last few days. I wanted to be happy and I think I succeeded in believing I was. But even this self-deception won't last as long as the devil's in me and I can't get rid of the guilt which is there. Deep down, darling, it's there. There's no explanation why I feel this way. Honesty had always been a virtue I priced greatly. It is as if I had broken a basic law of nature and nothing could put us right again. I am scared stiff of staying and destroying what we now have and then to have to let our future destroy the memory of our past.' He had whetted his guilt so fine that it had turned around and sliced him to pieces.

'Surely we could work this out together. I am no ogre waiting to pounce on you,' she said.

'If I think there is the slightest chance of it working, I would stay. But I know, Jacqueline. I hate it but I know. I have to get away from here, from England. I've thought a lot about it. I have made arrangement with Steve at work in case things don't work out with us. I will leave the company but keep my share of the business. You are financially independent of me, thank God. Do what you like with the house. I have no fixed plans but I heard there is a boat from Cape Town to Tristan de Cunha. I fancy taking that – as a starting point. I want to be irresponsible for a spell and drift with the tides.'

Here was the opportunity to fulfil his youthful dreams of travelling to the South Seas and other exotic places. But Tristan in the South Atlantic would make a good enough start. He no longer harboured ideals of paradises to be discovered, but he had to get away far and soon from Jacqueline or he might lose his courage and remain to eke out his days in self-distaste. His body would leave, must leave, but he knew he would be leaving his soul behind.

Jacqueline was stunned. She had not realized things had come to such a head. If Michael said he had thought about it, she knew he would have been thorough about it. She would not argue with it. How blind had she been if Michael had been pondering and planning on this departure for some time. Here was another failure in her life. Michael had been her mooring. She had not strayed afar in all these years. There was always him to get home to.

What a storm, so suddenly breaching the walls of her haven. But it was her duty to understand. She must allow him to go. She would not allow him to sacrifice his happiness to accommodate her own. That would be an injustice. She had to weather this. She had to – bloody hell!

'Jacqueline, Jacqueline,' Michael cried, enfolding her in his arms. 'Don't cry my darling, don't cry,' he pleaded, crying with her in her distress.

'Everything sounds so final. I had not expected this, Michael. I thought we would try to make things work again. If only we had talked more about it. Are we not worth another try?' she entreated. Crying was not her forte, but having started she found it impossible to stop.

She had not been one to dream and plan the future. She was too young for that when Gérard came along and swept her into this whirlwind called a future. Since he left she had taken life as it came and dealt with each period, the beginning and the end, as the inevitable, neither to be gloried in nor to be thrown into despair. But now she felt that what she had with Michael was what she might have dreamt of, what she might have been content with for the rest of her days. She had unknowingly lived a dream.

A relationship to her, however, must be one of consensus. When one party had decided to leave, there was no justification for the other to hold back the rein, to emotionally blackmail him to stay.

She disentangled herself from Michael, braced herself and told him, 'I won't make it difficult for you, I promise, but for today darling, let me cry.'

'After all,' she resumed, 'it is better to have someone to cry to, isn't it?' And the smile that followed broke his heart.

6 Holding the Reins

David had never known her to be weak. It was a revelation that she could cry. It was a revelation to see her break down over Michael's departure. She was human after all.

Michael had requested him to keep an eye on her but his spontaneous reaction was that she was well able to look after herself. Right until Michael left, she had been her usual amiable but controlled self. Indeed, she made it as casual and uneventful as she could. Then, when he was no longer there to see her, she went to pieces.

David was bewildered. He did not know how to respond to this sudden and unexpected feebleness of character. Neither of them had explained to him why Michael was going away. He guessed that it might be due to Michael's discovery about Carl some months ago. Perhaps he should not have mentioned Carl to Michael that day they were at *The Bull at Streatley*. Perhaps he had a little too much to drink. Perhaps…

Through this crack in Jacqueline's self-control, David realized the seriousness of the situation but not the whole substance of it. On the surface Michael and Jacqueline had remained the happily married couple and Jacqueline had helped to finalise Michael's trip to Tristan de Cunha. Now a role had opened up for him. For the first time she would be reliant on him, be dependent on him. Michael had conferred on him this task and he meant to embrace it with care and sensitivity.

The first two days after Michael had left, David came to see her each morning. She had rung Josh to say that she would be taking some time off. They would sit and have coffee and he might have a couple of toasts. They would talk of Michael but avoided the issue of his leaving. He would try to persuade her to eat something but she insisted she was not hungry.

The following days he would return in the afternoon and take her out for a spin in the country or he might stop at a pub and insisted that she had something to eat. Her tears moved him.

By the beginning of the following week, however, she had regained a degree of control and asked him to arrange for Josh to come over to see her. He had avoided getting to her office in case he ran into Denise and she, in her usual effusive manner, might corner him into a gossipy explanation. So he rang Josh and met him after work at the *Ferryboat* at Whitchurch to put him in the picture. He knew Josh held her in the highest regards and, being a private person himself, would appreciate and preserve her confidence.

The months went by and Josh took on more and more responsibility in running the business and did not let her down. They took on a new accounts executive to fulfil much of Josh's previous work-load as Jacqueline spent less and less time at the office and took several protracted trips abroad. Through this time David remained a close and available friend. After the second year, she travelled more locally in Europe until she found and decided to rent *Le Nid d'Or* at Lauzerte.

So what David had thought was a new beginning for the three of them at Pangbourne came quickly to an end. He knew they could not re-create the past for they had all changed and that youthful, charming exuberance of his Watford years had matured into a quieter but nonetheless gregarious affability which lifted the atmosphere whenever they were together. Michael's departure cut him. He would not analyse it but it cut him. He bore it alone. He felt it was unfair, cruel and inexplicable that Michael could have up and left him and Jacqueline. Michael had not offered him an explanation and he was too proud to ask for one. The dynamics had now changed. He had only Jacqueline to consider. It was a pre-occupation that made the situation bearable.

The weeks Jacqueline spent abroad at the beginning irked him. He had grown to depend on her presence as she had on his help. This symbiotic relationship existed independently of his marriage and his family life. That he could stay most of the week at Pangbourne facilitated this arrangement. When Jacqueline finally moved to Lauzerte, he had, by a process of slow accretion, taken on more responsibilities for her. She had found it morbid to have to return to the place where she had been happy only to be reminded of how unhappy she was. Once she had settled at Lauzerte, she would send for Josh a couple of times a year to go through the accounts of *Accent Recruitment*. And in later years she entrusted to David the sale of *Corner Oak* and the transfer of the company assets to her staff.

Those were patience testing days of lengthy waiting and brief encounters. As Gavin spent more time at Pangbourne and Judy took charge of the Barnet office, David felt quite at a loose end. Susan decided she would retire from teaching and went in the Barnet office two or three days a week to assist Judy and oversee the accounts. There was ample time on hand for David to play some golf and had a few drinks with friends at the Priest Hole, but his heart was not there. He had no reason and could not conjure up excuses often enough to go over to see Jacqueline in France. Michael had not been in touch and Jacqueline only did so when she needed him to handle her affairs in England and that too often through Josh.

At home he felt redundant all day long and even in the evening, when Susan was home and perhaps the children and their partners visited, he sensed he was the outsider looking in. He had been detached, dislocated from the train of family and his dearest friends. In this stasis he was the paralytic observer watching events unfolding around him.

On the few occasions he had met up with Jacqueline in France in recent years, he had the urge to throw up his life in England and get on Michael's old motorbike, that faithful jalopy he had inherited, and 'race' towards Lauzerte, presenting himself as a fait accompli at her doorsteps. He had debated this endlessly but could not find a legitimate excuse or the courage to desert his worthy wife and family.

Susan led a full social life, independent of him if required. Gavin and Judy had left home and, although they visited often, nucleated with Susan rather than with him. However, none of them had given him a justifiable cause to leave and cause disruption to the family unit.

His pre-occupation with Jacqueline would be inexplicable to others. She was not that pretty, younger woman who might have triggered off his mid-life crisis. She was older and in the eyes of his family and friends probably rather plain. That he could harbour a serious attraction for Jacqueline would be beyond their understanding. There would be a history that needed to be reluctantly unearthed, like a fox pursued, and a private gravitation to be made public. He could not expose his family to that. Staying on was a sacrifice he had to make for his family. Leaving them was a sacrifice he would have made for Jacqueline. He was torn.

There were moments of urgency when emotions welled within him whenever he was with her, when he swore he was going to do something about it. That was inevitably followed by months of a relaxed longing, of an ache almost muscular which was then easily assuaged by the comfort of indecision.

There had been no immediate conflict with Susan to initiate a break. The David, Michael, Jacqueline relationship was a simple and natural one to Susan. Michael was David's best friend at College and Jacqueline, who was Michael's girlfriend then, was now his wife. They had now separated and David was left in the middle, trying to handle both their affairs. Nothing could be more natural, according to Susan, except that this had gone on for too long. She could not understand how Jacqueline could keep on using David as a dog's body. She resented that.

Susan first met Jacqueline and Michael at Josh's wedding reception. She had taken to Michael straight away. He was urbane, well-spoken and mildly amusing. It was harder for her to see how David and he could have been such firm friends – there were chasms of class, of manner, of speech and of bearing between them. David exuded warmth and fun and openness – accessible. Michael was more reserved, wry and commanded respect, but appeared ready to be amused by David.

Jacqueline on the other hand was too difficult to read. She was friendly, ready to smile or laugh as the case required, but said very little. From a distance she was unexceptional. Close to, Susan could not consider her pretty. 'Spare' was the word that came to her mind – spare in curves, spare in beauty, spare in conversation, spare in allure. If anyone had told her that once Jacqueline was David's lover or that David was still besotted with her, Susan would have laughed out loud. 'Don't be silly,' she would have said decisively. Jacqueline was no challenge to her, just a slight irritation.

7 Journey On

A fury engulfed Jacqueline after David had kissed her before he left. She was awakened to the fact that David might have intentions towards her other than friendship and that she might have inadvertently encouraged him. If that was the case then it was an evil, evil thing she had done. Evil could exist without intention!

What on earth had she been doing with her life these past years? To be steeped for so long in desultory self-pity and in self-indulgence over the past was a grievous sin against the gift of existence. She blamed herself unequivocally for this. If she were religious, she would consider this lack of appreciation of the life given as a sin more mortal than the breaking of most Commandments.

'I'm going to get drunk. I am going to get bloody drunk,' she fumed, switched on suddenly to the vivid realisation of the waste she had allowed of her life. 'And when I wake up tomorrow I will clear this shitty existence aside. I will get out of this shit-hole I have dug for myself and wallowed in.'

And, in anger and self-disgust, she swore, 'Oh! God in heaven! Don't forgive me if don't straighten up my life. Just give me a little time.'

She walked out onto the balcony with a full glass of whisky and braved the cold evening air. The night was clear and into its wide expanse she raised her glass.

'I promise you, Michael, I promise you I will come out of this shitty rut,' she vowed. 'These wasted years, my darling, these wasted years – please forgive me.'

She turned around and headed back to her room.

'You'll be proud of me yet. You will, Michael, you will.'

Le Nid d'Or is now cleared of her things. Sophie from the Tourist office has agreed to store her belongings in her own garage. All her possessions in three large cardboard boxes besides what is in her travel case and a small backpack. When she returns to France she would clear away even more stuff. Possessions root deep like an establishment. She would free herself of them.

She has written to David explaining that she needs to get away and learn to breathe again. Some years ago when she met Susan at Josh's wedding, she could see how mutually suited they were. There was just a little possessiveness, a little mothering on her part, which Jacqueline found endearing and justified. David must stay where he is. To see too much of him would be dangling an unavailable carrot. That would not be fair.

She has decided it is time for a long trip to Australia and to Tasmania to see Clinger. It is surprising how much Clinger had always remained a watermark, pale but persistent, in Michael's and her life.

Later in the year she would like to go to China. The China she had read about was the China of Pearl S Buck[1] and Han Su Yin[2] and, from another book on Edward's shelves, Dream of the Red Chamber[3]. These were the fabrics on which were woven China's pasts. Each had offered a different texture, a different viewpoint from a different time. She wants to get to know Michael's China – the China that has re-blossomed, the China of today.

When she gets back from her travel, it would be time for her to settle down. She could not willingly go back to live near Pangbourne. She would buy a small cottage outside a village, perhaps not far from a small town in France. On a recent trip, driving in to Correze, she had been enchanted by Brive. It is a small town with all facilities close by. Turn into a lane or around a corner and you are likely to discover a restaurant, a bar or a small boutique. And the weekly markets are just her cup of tea.

---

[1] American writer and winner of both the Pulitzer and the Nobel Prize

[2] Chinese-born Eurasian writer famous for 'A Many-Splendoured Thing', 'The Crippled Tree' and 'My House Has Two Doors'

[3] 18th Century Chinese novel by Cao Xueqin, also known as The Story of The Stone

Not far away is the picturesque town of Tulle. She could easily spend many an afternoon browsing in *Librairie Préférences*, the town centre bookshop where, on a previous visit, she had bought a copy of *Cent Onze Haiku*[1] – a French translation beside the Japanese text of a selection of Bashō's[2] work.

She had been searching for a copy of Pangol's[3] play *Fanny* to complete the trilogy of *Marius, Fanny* and *César*. Apologising for not having it in stock, the gentleman who came to assist her had wisely suggested that she might be interested in *Cent Onze Haiku*. He explained briefly how he had first come across it and how much he had enjoyed it.

She was not familiar with Haiku but was immediately fascinated by its simplicity, its essence and its beauty, and was anxious to discover more. Now, she thought, if only her life could be so simplified with all its happiness, sorrow, love and despair poetically contained within a few words, encapsulated within three lines. A life not just condensed but distilled.

In a town or village where there is such a bookshop and such a knowledgeable assistant, she could easily live.

However, on the contrary, she could see herself in a small apartment in Central London, close to the

---

[1] Hundred and eleven Haiku. Haiku is a Japanese poem form of 17 syllables in 3 lines

[2] Bashō is a 17th Century Japanese poet famous for his Haiku

[3] Marcel Pangol. A French novelist, playwright and filmmaker.

theatres, the art galleries, the museums and the varied concerts that London famously hosts. How fortunate she feels to be in the position to choose the tracks she would follow, to be free from human ties, to be financially independent and to be physically and intellectually intact.

Once she has settled in, wherever that might turn out to be, she will think about voluntary work. On several occasions in France, she had spoken to homeless people and had always thought she might be able to be of help. Perhaps that is an avenue she could pursue. Maybe, gearing her energy towards others would free her from the energy spent on self-commiseration.

The previous night she had lit a fire in the garden incinerator and purposefully burnt old letters and most photographs and, severing that rusty, cumbersome chain to her past, the notebook which she had kept from the days with Edward. She had not written in it for years until her more recent encounter with Carl. That had to go.

She kept a picture taken by Lars, but she could not remember when. The three of them were sitting, inches deep in dry, curled leaves of burnt brown and gold, under a late autumnal beech. She was facing the camera and David and Michael sat leaning against her facing in opposite directions. The colours had faded a little and there was a dreamlike quality about it. She remembered Lars giving the photograph to her encased in a light faux leather frame. This she would take with her.

She wondered about Lars. He had talked of his love of skiing in the winter and exploring the Norwegian countryside in the summer. She wondered if he had the opportunity to travel far and wide around the world as he had hoped to do, and to fulfil his particular penchant to go on polar expeditions. There was always an element of the wilderness in him.

People meet and mostly they part never to know how life has meted out for each other. That is the way of the world. Make today matter.

Looking at David then, fresh, playful, uncomplicated, she would not have thought it possible that he would one day be the stalwart support he had afforded her in recent years. When Michael was no longer there she had fallen, in a depression, physically and mentally wrecked, into David's safety net. For that reason alone, now that she has gathered her composure, her health and mental faculties, she needs to let him go. He would be happiest with his wife and family even though he might not realize it. She feels certain that she has done the right thing. The intuitive urgency that she must release him somehow wakes her to the intuitive urgency of being part of the human race again.

Michael! Ah, Michael! Memories – for that is what has remained. Memories can fortify or they can destroy. We have to make our choice.

Even as she had fresh hopes of building their lives together again, sitting on the balcony that day he returned from China, she had already begun to lose him. He had not known it himself, but he was no longer able to reach and embrace the warmth emanating from her. And in the following days and months, she had stretched her hand out into an expanding emptiness. But the years she had shared with Michael have made her life worthwhile.

She no longer had any regrets that Michael had left. Each person must go and make a creation of his own life – like a piece of art.

'Make yours exquisite,' Michael, she whispered, 'make yours exquisite!' She straightened her back and felt invincible.

'*The Sandgrown'un – My Whispers*'– she had put that in her backpack. She'll take that on the plane with her. In the years that had passed, she had not taken courage to read it. Sufficient time has passed now for her to read it simply as another novel. Perhaps it might even be correct for her to send Carl a little comment on it. Carl had been sensible and not contacted her. He had got on with his life and written two more books, which he had not sent to her. '*The Sandgrown'un – My Whispers*' he had dedicated to Dorothy Reyes, his mother. It was the appropriate thing to do and she was proud of him.

Jacqueline checks her watch and walks through the house one more time, making sure the place is tidy and that she has not left anything behind. She goes out onto the balcony and from up high she feels she is ready to fly into that wide, wide world..

Even in the deepest woodland, through the harshest and longest winter, when spring comes at long last, out of the crisp dead leaves of the past, green shoots sprout.

Once again, she senses the stir of life.

8 Michael

A traffic jam is a traffic jam anywhere in the world and Michael knew from past experience that whichever route he takes on leaving Heathrow there is a likelihood of meeting a jam. He had slept well on the plane from Vientiane after a 2 weeks' stay. While visiting a temple there he had heard a Buddhist nun speaking in perfect English. Curiosity got the better of him and he approached her and discovered that, though originally from Laos, she was one of a small community of nuns and monks at the *Amaravati Monastery* at Hemel Hempstead in England. On 3 occasions they had conversed and Ajahn B had given him a contact name and telephone number for the Monastery.

On reaching England, he is now heading towards the monastery. He has decided not to make advance plans but to drop in and see how he might fit in there.

It would be a romantic notion to paraphrase his years of travelling as a search for some inner peace, or some truths or the meaning of life. It was no such thing. He had simply travelled on, found some places more interesting than others, and allowed circumstances to dictate where he would go next, because he could. More and more he had learned the futility of being stressed and how much more enriching the non-necessities of life outweighed the necessities.

The longest he had stayed at any one place was his visit to Don and Clinger in Tasmania three years before. He enjoyed mucking in with Don at the Dairy farm and sitting down in the early evening with them to dinner and, when Don had gone to bed, talking to Clinger about her four children. Lance, the eldest boy was a vet in a place whose name he could not pronounce in Queensland. Dean, the second son was a teacher in Adelaide and was married to Angel and they had 2 little girls. The youngest son, Jason, managed a small hotel at Hobart. Only Grace had remained in the farm. She was engaged to Toby, a worker at the farm and it was Clinger's hope that they would take over the business when Don retired.

Only once had Clinger asked about Jacqueline, and Michael had spoken as openly as only he could with Clinger, about how he still felt about Jacqueline. He had accepted the impossibility of their position, but had no regrets and no bitterness about it.

He had not once tried to contact Jacqueline. He trusted in her good sense and her strength of character to pull her through. He remembered her telling him long ago about how a perfume by way of enfleurage would instil its essence onto the user. He knew that the essence that is Jacqueline will remain with him for the rest of his life.

And now there is the possibility of a different kind of journey. He is not a religious person with established religious beliefs and tenets. He approaches Buddhism as a philosophy, a way of living and of being. It is an endless avenue towards tranquillity, and he has plenty of time to spare. Out there is a balance between nature and humanity. And on that journey of discovery he is about to step.

Acknowledgements

To Josh who first introduced me to the term *'Sandgrown'un'* at a business dinner in Blackpool.

To Andrew to whom I dedicate all references to perfumes. On my commenting on the effects of music on me, his response was that to him it was perfumes.

To Hélène Cavy, tutor at Open University Summer School at Caen, for whom *'Un Moment en l'Été'* was first written as homework.

To Dominique Medley for her advice on *'Un Moment en l'Été'*.

To The Open University for the little French I know which makes trips to France so much more fun.

To Gail Blackman who advised me on and scanned the picture for the front cover.

To Phil Ball for formatting the text for publication, for his IT and general advice and for his patience.

Printed in Great Britain
by Amazon